Amos B

The Sad Fortunes of the Revd Amos Barton

George Eliot

ET REMOTISSIMA PROPE

100 PAGES

100 PAGES

Published by Hesperus Press Limited

4 Rickett Street, London SW6 1RU

www.hesperuspress.com

First published in *Blackwood's Edinburgh Magazine* in 1857; published together with 'Mr Gilfil's Love-Story' and 'Janet's Repentance' as *Scenes of Clerical Life* in 1858. First published by Hesperus Press Limited, 2003

Foreword © Matthew Sweet, 2003

ISBN: 1-84391-051-9

CONTENTS

FOREWORD

In the autumn of 1856, Marian Evans – a journalist and
translator yet to try her hand at plot and dialogue or drag up in
her famous pseudonym – filed an article for the *Westminster
Review* on the state of modern British fiction. 'Silly Novels
by Lady Novelists' took half a dozen recent works by women
writers and squeezed them for their absurdities, popping
out examples of preposterous characterisation, overcooked
melodrama, flatulent prose, cack-handed engagement with
philosophical, political and doctrinal matters, and ignorance
of a life beyond the ballrooms of Belgravia.

'It is clear,' she reflected, considering the authors of
these works, 'that they write in elegant boudoirs, with violet-
coloured ink and a ruby pen; that they must be entirely
indifferent to publishers' accounts, and inexperienced in
every form of poverty except poverty of brains.' Her advice to
these dilettantes was simple. 'The severer critics are fulfilling
a chivalrous duty in depriving the mere fact of feminine
authorship of any false prestige which may give it a delusive
attraction, and in recommending women of mediocre faculties
– as at least a negative service they can render their sex – to
abstain from writing.' Ten days later, Evans took up her pen –
unencrusted with jewels, one presumes, and filled with
funereal black ink – and produced the opening lines of her
first work of narrative fiction. She called it 'The Sad Fortunes
of the Reverend Amos Barton', a title which came to her in a
state of semi-consciousness experienced in the Welsh seaside
resort of Tenby. It was published, unsigned, in the first 1857
number of *Blackwood's Edinburgh Magazine*. A year later,
it was collected under hard covers with two other novellas –
'Mr Gilfil's Love-Story' and 'Janet's Repentance' – as *Scenes of*

Clerical Life (1858). The name on the title page was George Eliot. Sober, masculine, and not remotely silly.

Amos Barton is a tale written against the kind of fiction derided in Eliot's journalism: distended tomes in which authors baffled their readers with phoney erudition, egged them on to become spoony over highly idealised protagonists, exhorted them to coo at the rodomontade of a melodramatic plot. That the story succeeds in avoiding these first two faults makes it fiction worth taking seriously; a manifesto for the rest of Eliot's literary career. Its persuasive power and tenacious life in the memory, however, are partly due to its failure in respect of the third.

Are we allowed to say such things about George Eliot? Not usually. Not since 1948, when F.R. Leavis claimed her for the select membership of his 'Great Tradition', and accorded her an honour from which her reputation has never quite recovered. In the twentieth century, no other Victorian novelist was treated with such wide-eyed, forelock-tugging deference. While many of her more populist contemporaries – Dickens, Trollope, Thackeray – began to be spoken of in seminar rooms and lecture halls with a kind of ironic detachment, Eliot was adopted by a generation of scholars who grew up with her as their idol, pin-up and role model. They were besotted by her aura of intellectual seriousness, thrilled by accounts of her staying up all night to read German critical theory, identified with her professional single-mindedness and cultural appetites, bought postcards of her to put by their desks. They studied her work through the contemporary discourses she absorbed – Darwinism, Comtean positivism, phrenology, biology and geology – and paid less attention to its sensational pleasures.

Eliot, for all her avowed distaste for melodrama, could not

completely resist its influence. *Middlemarch* (1872) has its scenes around the microscope, but it also has a blackmail plot at which Mrs Henry Wood would not have thumbed her nose. *Daniel Deronda* (1876) offers a tough debate on the progress of the Zionist movement, but the novel is led by a social-climbing, roulette-playing heroine who would have had little problem holding her own on the pages of a Mary Elizabeth Braddon three-decker. Eliot has more in common with these contemporaries – whose work severer critics often dismissed as silly – than it has been customary to acknowledge. *Amos Barton*, for example, despite its rejection of sensational incident, turns on the possibility that a curate, his wife, and an impecunious countess of dubious morals have formed a *ménage à trois* in rural Warwickshire – just the kind of scandal that had been providing copy for the *News of the World* since 1843.

One of the works Eliot subjects to brisk murder in 'Silly Novels by Lady Novelists' is *The Old Grey Church*. Although the title page makes no such admission, reviewers would have known that the book was the work of the Honourable Caroline Lucy, composer of aristocratic romances and biblically themed children's puzzle books. Its plot – which Eliot considered a 'drivelling narrative, which, like a bad drawing, represents nothing' – relates how the heroine rejects the romantic attentions of a rakish baronet in favour of a young clergyman whose manners are as pristine as his dog-collar. It is the story of a romantic triangle in clerical circles. So, too, in its own way, is *Amos Barton*.

The clergyman at the centre of Eliot's story is, the narrator insists, unlike the hero of the more sensational or sappy stories its author was required to review. Barton is presented to us as 'a man whose virtues were not heroic, and who had no undetected crime within his breast; who had not the slightest mystery hanging about him, but was palpably and unmistakably commonplace'. And yet mystery does hang about him. He fails to register its power – he wanders oblivious through the plot like a blindfolded Harold Lloyd tripping from girder to swinging girder – but it is present. Who is the cash-strapped aristocrat whom the curate has invited into the spare bedroom? Was the man with whom she was formerly living really her brother? What is Mrs Barton's attitude to their unusual lodger? Does the old clergyman truly, as his neighbours suspect, pop into the Countess' boudoir to help her lace her boots? The Revd Amos Barton has no nose for a sensation – that, indeed, is one of his most serious flaws – but the reader suffers no such deficit. So we can enjoy both the progress of the scandal and reflect upon its melancholy consequences – and George Eliot can have her cake and eat it.

– *Matthew Sweet, 2003*

Amos Barton

Shepperton Church was a very different-looking building five and twenty years ago. To be sure, its substantial stone tower looks at you through its intelligent eye, the clock, with the friendly expression of former days, but in everything else what changes! Now there is a wide span of slated roof flanking the old steeple; the windows are tall and symmetrical; the outer doors are resplendent with oak-graining, the inner doors reverentially noiseless with a garment of red baize; and the walls, you are convinced, no lichen will ever again effect a settlement on – they are smooth and innutrient as the summit of the Revd Amos Barton's head, after ten years of baldness and supererogatory soap. Pass through the baize doors and you will see the nave filled with well-shaped benches, understood to be free seats, while in certain eligible corners, less directly under the fire of the clergyman's eye, there are pews reserved for the Shepperton gentility. Ample galleries are supported on iron pillars, and in one of them stands the crowning glory, the very clasp or aigrette of Shepperton Church adornment – namely, an organ, not very much out of repair, on which a collector of small rents, differentiated by the force of circumstances into an organist, will accompany the alacrity of your departure after the blessing, by a sacred minuet or an easy Gloria.

'Immense improvement!' says the well-regulated mind, which unintermittingly rejoices in the New Police, the Tithe Commutation Act, the penny-post, and all guarantees of human advancement,[1] and has no moments when conservative-reforming intellect takes a nap, while imagination does a little Toryism by the sly, revelling in regret that dear old brown, crumbling, picturesque inefficiency is everywhere giving place to spick-and-span new-painted, new-varnished efficiency, which will yield endless diagrams, plans, elevations, and sections, but alas! no picture. Mine, I fear, is not a well-regulated mind; it has an occasional tenderness for old abuses; it lingers with a certain fondness over the days of nasal clerks and top-booted parsons, and has a sigh for the departed shades of vulgar errors. So it is not surprising that I recall with a fond sadness Shepperton Church as it was in the old days, with its outer coat of rough stucco, its red-tiled roof, its heterogeneous windows patched with desultory bits of painted glass, and its little flight of steps with their wooden rail running up the outer wall and leading to the schoolchildren's gallery.

Then inside, what dear old quaintnesses! which I began to look at with delight, even when I was so crude a member of the congregation that my nurse found it necessary to provide for the reinforcement of my devotional patience by smuggling bread and butter into the sacred edifice. There was the chancel, guarded by two little cherubim looking uncomfortably squeezed between arch and wall, and adorned with the escutcheons of the Oldinport family, which showed me inexhaustible possibilities of meaning in their blood-red hands, their death's heads and crossbones, their leopards' paws, and Maltese crosses. There were inscriptions on the panels of the singing-gallery, telling of benefactions to the poor of Shepperton, with an involuted elegance of capitals and final flourishes, which my alphabetic erudition traced with ever-new delight. No benches in those days, but huge roomy pews, round which devout churchgoers sat during 'lessons', trying to look anywhere else than into each other's eyes. No low partitions, allowing you, with a dreary absence of contrast and mystery, to see everything at all moments; but tall dark panels, under whose shadow I sank with a sense of retirement through

4

the Litany, only to feel with more intensity my burst into the conspicuousness of public life when I was made to stand up on the seat during the psalms or the singing.

And the singing was no mechanical affair of official routine; it had a drama. As the moment of psalmody approached, by some process to me as mysterious and untraceable as the opening of the flowers or the breaking-out of the stars, a slate appeared in front of the gallery, advertising in bold characters the psalm about to be sung, lest the sonorous announcement of the clerk should still leave the bucolic mind in doubt on that head. Then followed the migration of the clerk to the gallery, where, in company with a bassoon, two key-bugles, a carpenter understood to have an amazing power of singing 'counter', and two lesser musical stars, he formed the complement of a choir regarded in Shepperton as one of distinguished attraction, occasionally known to draw hearers from the next parish. The innovation of hymn books was as yet undreamt of; even the New Version was regarded with a sort of melancholy tolerance, as part of the common degeneracy in a time when prices had dwindled, and a cotton gown was no longer stout enough to last a lifetime; for the lyrical taste of the best heads in Shepperton had been formed on Sternhold and Hopkins.[2] But the greatest triumphs of the Shepperton choir were reserved for the Sundays when the slate announced an 'Anthem', with a dignified abstinence from particularisation, both words and music lying far beyond the reach of the most ambitious amateur in the congregation – an anthem in which the key-bugles always ran away at a great pace, while the bassoon every now and then boomed a flying shot after them.

As for the clergyman, Mr Gilfil, an excellent old gentleman who smoked very long pipes and preached very short sermons, I must not speak of him or I might be tempted to tell the story of his life, which had its little romance, as most lives have between the ages of teetotum and tobacco. And at present I am concerned with quite another sort of clergyman: the Revd Amos Barton, who did not come to Shepperton until long after Mr Gilfil had departed this life – until after an interval in which Evangelicalism and the Catholic Question[3] had begun to agitate the rustic mind with controversial debates. A Popish blacksmith had produced a strong Protestant reaction by declaring that as soon as the Emancipation Bill was passed he should do a great stroke of business in gridirons; and the disinclination of the Shepperton parishioners generally to dim the unique glory of St Lawrence[4] rendered the Church and Constitution an affair of their business and bosoms. A zealous Evangelical preacher had made the old sounding board vibrate with quite a different sort of elocution from Mr Gilfil's; the hymn book had almost superseded the Old and New Versions; and the great square pews were crowded with new faces from distant corners of the parish – perhaps from dissenting chapels.

You are not imagining, I hope, that Amos Barton was the incumbent of Shepperton. He was no such thing. Those were days when a man could hold three small livings, starve a curate apiece on two of them, and live badly himself on the third. It was so with the vicar of Shepperton; a vicar given to bricks and mortar, and thereby running into debt far away in a northern county – who executed his vicarial functions towards Shepperton by pocketing the sum of thirty-five pounds ten per annum, the net surplus remaining to him from the proceeds of that living, after the disbursement of eighty pounds as the annual stipend of his curate. And now, pray, can you solve me the following problem? Given a man with a wife and six children: let him be obliged always to exhibit himself when outside his own door in a suit of black broadcloth, such as will not undermine the foundations of the Establishment by a paltry plebeian glossiness or an unseemly whiteness at the edges; in a snowy cravat, which is a serious investment of labour in the hemming, starching, and ironing departments; and in a hat which shows no symptom of taking to the hideous doctrine of expediency, and shaping itself according to circumstances; let him have a parish large enough to create an external necessity for abundant shoe-leather, and an internal necessity for abundant beef and mutton, as well as poor enough to require frequent priestly consolation in the shape of shillings and sixpences; and, lastly, let him be compelled, by his own pride and other people's, to dress his wife and children with gentility from bonnet-strings to shoestrings. By what process of division can the sum of eighty pounds per annum be made to yield a quotient which will cover that man's weekly expenses? This was the problem presented by the position of the Revd Amos Barton, as curate of Shepperton, rather more than twenty years ago.

What was thought of this problem, and of the man who had to work it out, by some of the well-to-do inhabitants of Shepperton, two years or more after Mr Barton's arrival among them, you shall hear, if you will accompany me to Cross Farm, and to the fireside of Mrs Patten, a childless old lady, who had got rich chiefly by the negative process of spending nothing. Mrs Patten's passive accumulation of wealth, through all sorts of 'bad times' on the farm of which she had been sole tenant since her husband's death, her epigrammatic neighbour, Mrs Hackit, sarcastically accounted for by supposing that 'sixpences grew on the bents of Cross Farm'; while Mr Hackit, expressing his views more literally, reminded his wife that 'money breeds money'. Mr and Mrs Hackit, from the neighbouring farm, are Mrs Patten's guests this evening; so is Mr Pilgrim, the doctor from the nearest market town, who, though occasionally affecting aristocratic airs, and giving late dinners with enigmatic side dishes and poisonous port, is never so comfortable as when he is relaxing his professional legs in one of those excellent farmhouses where the mice are sleek and the mistress sickly. And he is at this moment in clover.

For the flickering of Mrs Patten's bright fire is reflected in her bright copper tea-kettle, the home-made muffins glisten with an inviting succulence, and Mrs Patten's niece, a single lady of fifty, who has refused the most ineligible offers out of devotion to her aged aunt, is pouring the rich cream into the fragrant tea with a discreet liberality.

Reader! *did* you ever taste such a cup of tea as Miss Gibbs is this moment handing to Mr Pilgrim? Do you know the dulcet strength, the animating blandness of tea sufficiently blended with real farmhouse cream? No – most likely you are a miserable town-bred reader who thinks of cream as a thinnish white fluid, delivered in infinitesimal pennyworths down area steps; or perhaps, from a presentiment of calves' brains, you refrain from any lacteal addition, and rasp your tongue with unmitigated bohea. You have a vague idea of a milch cow as probably a white-plaster animal standing in a butterman's window, and you know nothing of the sweet history of genuine cream, such as Miss Gibbs's: how it was this morning in the udders of the large sleek beasts as they stood lowing a patient entreaty under the milking-shed; how it fell with a pleasant rhythm into Betty's pail, sending a delicious incense into the cool air; how it was carried into that temple of moist cleanliness, the dairy, where it quietly separated itself from the meaner elements of milk, and lay in mellowed whiteness, ready for the skimming-dish which transferred it to Miss Gibbs's glass cream-jug. If I am right in my conjecture, you are unacquainted with the highest possibilities of tea, and Mr Pilgrim, who is holding that cup in his hands, has an idea beyond you.

Mrs Hackit declines cream; she has so long abstained from it with an eye to the weekly butter-money that abstinence, wedded to habit, has begotten aversion. She is a thin woman with a chronic liver complaint, which would have secured her Mr Pilgrim's entire regard and unreserved good word, even if he had not been in awe of her tongue, which was as sharp as his own lancet. She has brought her knitting – no frivolous fancy knitting, but a substantial woollen stocking; the click-click of her knitting needles is the running accompaniment to all her conversation, and in her utmost enjoyment of spoiling a friend's self-satisfaction, she was never known to spoil a stocking.

Mrs Patten does not admire this excessive click-clicking activity. Quiescence in an easy chair, under the sense of compound interest perpetually accumulating, has long seemed an ample function to her, and she does her malevolence gently. She is a pretty little old woman of eighty, with a close cap and tiny flat white curls round her face, as natty and unsoiled and invariable as the waxen image of a little old lady under a glass case; once a lady's maid, and married for her beauty. She used to adore her husband, and now she adores her money, cherishing a quiet blood-relation's hatred for her niece, Janet Gibbs, who, she knows, expects a large legacy, and whom she is determined to disappoint. Her money shall all go in a lump to a distant relation of her husband's, and Janet shall be saved the trouble of pretending to cry by finding that she is left with a miserable pittance.

Mrs Patten has more respect for her neighbour, Mr Hackit, than for most people. Mr Hackit is a shrewd, substantial man, whose advice about crops is always worth listening to, and who is too well off to want to borrow money.

And now that we are snug and warm with this little tea party, while it is freezing with February bitterness outside, we will listen to what they are talking about.

'So,' said Mr Pilgrim, with his mouth only half empty of muffin, 'you had a row in Shepperton Church last Sunday. I was at Jim Hood's, the bassoon-man's, this morning, attending his wife, and he swears he'll be revenged on the parson – a confounded, methodistical, meddlesome chap who must be putting his finger in every pie. What was it all about?'

'O, a passill o' nonsense,' said Mr Hackit, sticking one thumb between the buttons of his capacious waistcoat, and retaining a pinch of snuff with the other – for he was but moderately given to 'the cups that cheer but not inebriate',[5] and had already finished his tea. 'They began to sing the wedding psalm[6] for a new-married couple, as pretty a psalm an' as pretty a tune as any in the Prayer Book. It's been sung for every new-married couple since I was a boy. And what can be better?' Here Mr Hackit stretched out his left arm, threw back his head, and broke into melody –

> *'Oh what a happy thing it is,*
> *And joyful for to see,*
> *Brethren to dwell together in*
> *Friendship and unity.*

'But Mr Barton is all for the hymns, and a sort o' music as I can't join in at all.'

'And so,' said Mr Pilgrim, recalling Mr Hackit from lyrical

reminiscences to narrative, 'he called out "Silence!" did he, when he got into the pulpit, and gave a hymn out himself to some meeting-house tune?'

'Yes,' said Mrs Hackit, stooping towards the candle to pick up a stitch, 'and turned as red as a turkeycock. I often say, when he preaches about meekness, he gives himself a slap in the face. He's like me – he's got a temper of his own.'

'Rather a low-bred fellow, I think, Barton,' said Mr Pilgrim, who hated the Revd Amos for two reasons: because he had called in a new doctor, recently settled in Shepperton; and because, being himself a dabbler in drugs, he had the credit of having cured a patient of Mr Pilgrim's. 'They say his father was a dissenting shoemaker, and he's half a dissenter himself. Why, doesn't he preach extempore in that cottage up here, of a Sunday evening?'

'Tchaw!' – this was Mr Hackit's favourite interjection – 'that preaching without book's no good, only when a man has a gift, and has the Bible at his fingers' ends. It was all very well for Parry – he'd a gift, and in my youth I've heard the Ranters[7] out o' doors in Yorkshire go on for an hour or two on end, without ever sticking fast a minute. There was one clever chap, I remember, as used to say, "You're like the woodpigeon: it says 'Do, do, do,' all day, and never sets about any work itself." That's bringing it home to people. But our parson's no gift at all that way. He can preach as good a sermon as need be heard when he writes it down. But when he tries to preach wi'out book, he rambles about, and doesn't stick to his text, and every now and then he flounders about like a sheep as has cast itself and can't get on its legs again. You wouldn't like that, Mrs Patten, if you was to go to church now?'

'Eh, dear,' said Mrs Patten, falling back in her chair, and lifting up her little withered hands, 'what 'ud Mr Gilfil say if he was worthy to know the changes as have come about i' the Church these last ten years? I don't understand these new sort o' doctrines. When Mr Barton comes to see me, he talks about nothing but my sins and my need o' marcy. Now, Mr Hackit, I've never been a sinner. From the fust beginning, when I went into service, I al'ys did my duty by my emplyers. I was a good wife as any in the county – never aggravated my husband. The cheese-factor used to say my cheese was al'ys to be depended on. I've known women, as their cheeses swelled a shame to be seen, when their husbands had counted on the cheese-money to make up their rent; and yet they'd three gowns to my one. If I'm not to be saved, I know a many as are in a bad way. But it's well for me as I can't go to church any longer, for if th' old singers are to be done away with, there'll be nothing left as it was in Mr Patten's time. And what's more, I hear you've settled to pull the church down and build it up new?'

Now the fact was that the Revd Amos Barton, on his last visit to Mrs Patten, had urged her to enlarge her promised subscription of twenty pounds, representing to her that she was only a steward of her riches, and that she could not spend them more for the glory of God than by giving a heavy subscription towards the rebuilding of Shepperton Church – a practical precept which was not likely to smooth the way to her acceptance of his theological doctrine. Mr Hackit, who had more doctrinal enlightenment than Mrs Patten, had been a little shocked by the heathenism of her speech, and was glad of the new turn given to the subject by this question, addressed to him as churchwarden and an authority in all parochial matters.

'Ah,' he answered, 'the parson's bothered us into it at last, and we're to begin pulling down this spring. But we haven't got money enough yet. I was for waiting till we'd made up the sum, and, for my part, I think the congregation's fell off o' late; though Mr Barton says that's because there's been no room for the people when they've come. You see, the congregation got so large in Parry's time, the people stood in the aisles; but there's never any crowd now, as I can see.'

'Well,' said Mrs Hackit, whose good nature began to act now that it was a little in contradiction with the dominant tone of the conversation, '*I* like Mr Barton. I think he's a good sort o' man, for all he's not overburden'd i' th' upper storey, and his wife's as nice a ladylike woman as I'd wish to see. How nice she keeps her children! and little enough money to do't with. And a delicate creatur' – six children, and another a-coming. I don't know how they make both ends meet, I'm sure, now her aunt has left 'em. But I sent 'em a cheese and a sack o' potatoes last week; that's something towards filling the little mouths.'

'Ah!' said Mr Hackit, 'and my wife makes Mr Barton a good stiff glass o' brandy and water when he comes into supper after his cottage preaching. The parson likes it; it puts a bit o' colour into his face, and makes him look a deal handsomer.'

This allusion to brandy and water suggested to Miss Gibbs the introduction of the liquor decanters, now that the tea was cleared away; for in bucolic society five and twenty years ago, the human animal of the male sex was understood to be perpetually athirst, and 'something to drink' was as necessary a 'condition of thought' as Time and Space.

'Now, that cottage preaching,' said Mr Pilgrim, mixing himself a strong glass of 'cold without', 'I was talking about it to our Parson Ely the other day, and he doesn't approve of it at all. He said it did as much harm as good to give a too familiar aspect to religious teaching. That was what Ely said – it does as much harm as good to give a too familiar aspect to religious teaching.'

Mr Pilgrim generally spoke with an intermittent kind of splutter; indeed, one of his patients had observed that it was a pity such a clever man had a ' 'pediment' in his speech. But when he came to what he conceived the pith of his argument or the point of his joke, he mouthed out his words with slow emphasis – as a hen, when advertising her *accouchement*, passes at irregular intervals from pianissimo semiquavers to fortissimo crotchets. He thought this speech of Mr Ely's particularly metaphysical and profound, and the more decisive of the question because it was a generality which represented no particulars to his mind.

'Well, I don't know about that,' said Mrs Hackit, who had always the courage of her opinion, 'but I know some of our labourers and stockingers, as used never to come to church, come to the cottage, and that's better than never hearing anything good from week's end to week's end. And there's that Track Society[8] as Mr Barton has begun – I've seen more o' the poor people with going tracking than all the time I've lived in the parish before. And there'd need be something done among 'em, for the drinking at them Benefit Clubs is shameful. There's hardly a steady man or steady woman either but what's a dissenter.'

During this speech of Mrs Hackit's, Mr Pilgrim had emitted a succession of little snorts, something like the treble grunts of a guinea pig, which were always with him the sign of suppressed disapproval. But he never contradicted Mrs Hackit – a woman whose 'potluck' was always to be relied on, and who, on her side, had unlimited reliance on bleeding, blistering, and draughts.

Mrs Patten, however, felt equal disapprobation, and had no reasons for suppressing it.

'Well,' she remarked, 'I've heared of no good from

interfering with one's neighbours, poor or rich. And I hate the sight o' women going about trapesing from house to house in all weathers, wet or dry, and coming in with their petticoats dagged and their shoes all over mud. Janet wanted to join in the tracking, but I told her I'd have nobody tracking out o' my house; when I'm gone, she may do as she likes. I never dagged my petticoats in *my* life, and I've no opinion o' that sort o' religion.'

'No,' said Mr Hackit, who was fond of soothing the acerbities of the feminine mind with a jocose compliment, 'you held your petticoats so high, to show your tight ankles: it isn't everybody as likes to show her ankles.'

This joke met with general acceptance, even from the snubbed Janet, whose ankles were only tight in the sense of looking extremely squeezed by her boots. But Janet seemed always to identify herself with her aunt's personality, holding her own under protest.

Under cover of the general laughter the gentlemen replenished their glasses, Mr Pilgrim attempting to give his the character of a stirrup-cup by observing that he 'must be going'. Miss Gibbs seized this opportunity of telling Mrs Hackit that she suspected Betty, the dairymaid, of frying the best bacon for the shepherd when he sat up with her to 'help brew'; whereupon Mrs Hackit replied that she had always thought Betty false; and Mrs Patten said there was no bacon stolen when *she* was able to manage. Mr Hackit, who often complained that he 'never saw the like to women with their maids – he never had any trouble with his men', avoided listening to this discussion by raising the question of vetches with Mr Pilgrim. The stream of conversation had thus diverged, and no more was said about the Revd Amos Barton, who is the main object of interest to us just now. So we may leave Cross Farm without waiting till Mrs Hackit, resolutely donning her clogs and wrappings, renders it incumbent on Mr Pilgrim also to fulfil his frequent threat of going.

2

It was happy for the Revd Amos Barton that he did not, like us, overhear the conversation recorded in the last chapter. Indeed, what mortal is there of us who would find his satisfaction enhanced by an opportunity of comparing the picture he presents to himself of his own doings with the picture they make on the mental retina of his neighbours? We are poor plants buoyed up by the air-vessels of our own conceit: alas for us if we get a few pinches that empty us of that windy self-subsistence! The very capacity for good would go out of us. For, tell the most impassioned orator, suddenly, that his wig is awry, or his shirt-lap hanging out, and that he is tickling people by the oddity of his person, instead of thrilling them by the energy of his periods, and you would infallibly dry up the spring of his eloquence. That is a deep and wide saying, that no miracle can be wrought without faith – without the worker's faith in himself, as well as the recipient's faith in him. And the greater part of the worker's faith in himself is made up of the faith that others believe in him.

Let me be persuaded that my neighbour Jenkins considers me a blockhead, and I shall never shine in conversation with him any more. Let me discover that the lovely Phoebe thinks my squint intolerable, and I shall never be able to fix her blandly with my disengaged eye again. Thank Heaven, then, that a little illusion is left to us to enable us to be useful and agreeable – that we don't know exactly what our friends think of us – that the world is not made of looking glass to show us just the figure we are making, and just what is going on behind our backs! By the help of dear friendly illusion, we are able to dream that we are charming and our faces wear a becoming air of self-possession; we are able to dream that other men admire our talents – and our benignity is undisturbed; we are able to dream that we are doing much good – and we do a little.

Thus it was with Amos Barton on that very Thursday evening when he was the subject of the conversation at Cross Farm. He had been dining at Mr Farquhar's, the secondary squire of the parish, and, stimulated by unwonted gravies and port-wine, had been delivering his opinion on affairs parochial and extra-parochial with considerable animation. And he was now returning home in the moonlight – a little chill, it is true, for he had just now no greatcoat compatible with clerical dignity, and a fur boa round one's neck, with a waterproof cape over one's shoulders, doesn't frighten away the cold from one's legs; but entirely unsuspicious, not only of Mr Hackit's estimate of his oratorical powers, but also of the critical remarks passed on him by the Misses Farquhar as soon as the drawing-room door had closed behind him. Miss Julia had observed that she *never* heard anyone sniff so frightfully as Mr Barton did – she had a great mind to offer him her pocket handkerchief; and Miss Arabella wondered why he always said he was going *for* to do a thing. He, excellent man! was meditating fresh pastoral exertions on the morrow. He would set on foot his lending library in which he had introduced some books that would be a pretty sharp blow to the Dissenters – one especially, purporting to be written by a working man who, out of pure zeal for the welfare of his class, took the trouble to warn them in this way against those hypocritical thieves, the Dissenting preachers. The Revd

Amos Barton profoundly believed in the existence of that working man, and had thoughts of writing to him. Dissent, he considered, would have its head bruised in Shepperton, for did he not attack it in two ways? He preached Low-Church doctrine – as evangelical as anything to be heard in the Independent Chapel, and he made a High-Church assertion of ecclesiastical powers and functions. Clearly, the Dissenters would feel that 'the parson' was too many for them. Nothing like a man who combines shrewdness with energy. The wisdom of the serpent, Mr Barton considered, was one of his strong points.

Look at him as he winds through the little churchyard! The silver light that falls aslant on church and tomb enables you to see his slim black figure, made all the slimmer by tight pantaloons, as it flits past the pale gravestones. He walks with a quick step, and is now rapping with sharp decision at the vicarage door. It is opened without delay by the nurse, cook, and housemaid, all at once – that is to say, by the robust maid-of-all-work, Nanny; and as Mr Barton hangs up his hat in the passage, you see that a narrow face of no particular complexion – even the smallpox that has attacked it seems to have been of a mongrel, indefinite kind – with features of no particular shape, and an eye of no particular expression, is surmounted by a slope of baldness gently rising from brow to crown. You judge him, rightly, to be about forty. The house is quiet, for it is half-past ten, and the children have long been gone to bed. He opens the sitting-room door, but instead of seeing his wife, as he expected, stitching with the nimblest of fingers by the light of one candle, he finds her dispensing with the light of a candle altogether. She is softly pacing up and down by the red firelight, holding in her arms little Walter, the year-old baby, who looks over her shoulder with large

18

wide-open eyes, while the patient mother pats his back with her soft hand, and glances with a sigh at the heap of large and small stockings lying unmended on the table.

She was a lovely woman – Mrs Amos Barton, a large, fair, gentle madonna with thick, close, chestnut curls beside her well-rounded cheeks, and with large, tender, short-sighted eyes. The flowing lines of her tall figure made the limpest dress look graceful, and her old frayed black silk seemed to repose on her bust and limbs with a placid elegance and sense of distinction, in strong contrast with the uneasy sense of being no fit that seemed to express itself in the rustling of Mrs Farquhar's *gros de Naples*[9]. The caps she wore would have been pronounced, when off her head, utterly heavy and hideous – for in those days even fashionable caps were large and floppy; but surmounting her long arched neck, and mingling their borders of cheap lace and ribbon with her chestnut curls, they seemed miracles of successful millinery. Among strangers she was shy and tremulous as a girl of fifteen; she blushed crimson if anyone appealed to her opinion; yet that tall, graceful, substantial presence was so imposing in its mildness that men spoke to her with an agreeable sensation of timidity. Soothing, unspeakable charm of gentle womanhood! which supersedes all acquisitions, all accomplishments. You would never have asked, at any period of Mrs Amos Barton's life, if she sketched or played the piano. You would even perhaps have been rather scandalised if she had descended from the serene dignity of *being* to the assiduous unrest of *doing*. Happy the man, you would have thought, whose eye will rest on her in the pauses of his fireside reading – whose hot aching forehead will be soothed by the contact of her cool soft hand – who will recover himself from dejection at his mistakes and failures in the loving light of her unreproaching eyes! You would not, perhaps, have anticipated that this bliss would fall to the share of precisely such a man as Amos Barton whom you have already surmised not to have the refined sensibilities for which you might have imagined Mrs Barton's qualities to be destined by pre-established harmony. But I, for one, do not grudge Amos Barton his sweet wife. I have all my life had a sympathy for mongrel ungainly dogs, who are nobody's pets, and I would rather surprise one of them by a pat and a pleasant morsel than meet the condescending advances of the loveliest Skye terrier who has his cushion by my lady's chair. That, to be sure, is not the way of the world: if it happens to see a fellow of fine proportions and aristocratic mien, who makes no faux pas, and wins golden opinions from all sorts of men, it straight away picks out for him the loveliest of unmarried women, and says, '*There* would be a proper match!' Not at all, say I: let that successful, well-shapen, discreet and able gentleman put up with something less than the best in the matrimonial department, and let the sweet woman go to make sunshine and a soft pillow for the poor devil whose legs are not models, whose efforts are often blunders, and who in general gets more kicks than halfpence. She – the sweet woman – will like it as well, for her sublime capacity of loving will have all the more scope; and I venture to say, Mrs Barton's nature would never have grown half so angelic if she had married the man you would perhaps have had in your eye for her – a man with sufficient income and abundant personal éclat. Besides, Amos was an affectionate husband, and, in his way, valued his wife as his best treasure.

But now he has shut the door behind him, and said, 'Well, Milly!'

'Well, dear!' was the corresponding greeting, made eloquent by a smile.

'So that young rascal won't go to sleep! Can't you give him to Nanny?'

'Why, Nanny has been busy ironing this evening; but I think I'll take him to her now.' And Mrs Barton glided towards the kitchen while her husband ran upstairs to put on his maize-coloured dressing-gown, in which costume he was quietly filling his long pipe when his wife returned to the sitting-room.

Maize is a colour that decidedly did not suit his complexion, and it is one that soon soils; why, then, did Mr Barton select it for domestic wear? Perhaps because he had a knack of hitting on the wrong thing in garb as well as in grammar.

Mrs Barton now lit her candle, and seated herself before her heap of stockings. She had something disagreeable to tell her husband, but she would not enter on it at once.

'Have you had a nice evening, dear?'

'Yes, pretty well. Ely was there to dinner, but went away rather early. Miss Arabella is setting her cap at him with a vengeance. But I don't think he's much smitten. I've a notion Ely's engaged to someone at a distance, and will astonish all the ladies who are languishing for him here by bringing home his bride one of these days. Ely's a sly dog, he'll like that.'

'Did the Farquhars say anything about the singing last Sunday?'

'Yes, Farquhar said he thought it was time there was some improvement in the choir. But he was rather scandalised at my setting the tune of "Lydia". He says he's always hearing it as he passes the Independent meeting.' Here Mr Barton laughed – he had a way of laughing at criticisms that other people thought damaging – and thereby showed the remainder of a set of teeth which, like the remnants of the Old Guard, were few in number, and very much the worse for wear. 'But,' he continued, 'Mrs Farquhar talked the most about Mr Bridmain and the Countess. She has taken up all the gossip about them, and wanted to convert me to her opinion, but I told her pretty strongly what I thought.'

'Dear me! Why will people take so much pains to find out evil about others? I have had a note from the Countess since you went, asking us to dine with them on Friday.' Here Mrs Barton reached the note from the mantelpiece, and gave it to her husband. We will look over his shoulder while he reads it:

Sweetest Milly,
Bring your lovely face with your husband to dine with us
on Friday at seven – do. If not, I will be sulky with you till
Sunday when I shall be obliged to see you, and shall long to
kiss you that very moment. Yours, according to your answer,
Caroline Czerlaski

'Just like her, isn't it?' said Mrs Barton. 'I suppose we can go?'

'Yes, I have no engagement. The Clerical Meeting is tomorrow, you know.'

'And, dear, Woods the butcher called, to say he must have some money next week. He has a payment to make up.'

This announcement made Mr Barton thoughtful. He puffed more rapidly, and looked at the fire.

'I think I must ask Hackit to lend me twenty pounds, for it is nearly two months till Lady Day, and we can't give Woods our last shilling.'

'I hardly like you to ask Mr Hackit, dear – he and Mrs Hackit have been so very kind to us; they have sent us so many things lately.'

'Then I must ask Oldinport. I'm going to write to him

tomorrow morning, for to tell him the arrangement I've been thinking of about having service in the workhouse while the church is being enlarged. If he agrees to attend service there once or twice, the other people will come. Net the large fish, and you're sure to have the small fry.'

'I wish we could do without borrowing money, and yet I don't see how we can. Poor Fred must have some new shoes. I couldn't let him go to Mrs Bond's yesterday because his toes were peeping out, dear child! and I can't let him walk anywhere except in the garden. He must have a pair before Sunday. Really, boots and shoes are the greatest trouble of my life. Everything else one can turn and turn about, and make old look like new; but there's no coaxing boots and shoes to look better than they are.'

Mrs Barton was playfully undervaluing her skill in metamorphosing boots and shoes. She had at that moment on her feet a pair of slippers which had long ago lived through the prunella phase of their existence, and were now running a respectable career as black silk slippers, having been neatly covered with that material by Mrs Barton's own neat fingers. Wonderful fingers those! They were never empty, for if she went to spend a few hours with a friendly parishioner, out came her thimble and a piece of calico or muslin, which, before she left, had become a mysterious little garment with all sorts of hemmed ins and outs. She was even trying to persuade her husband to leave off tight pantaloons, because if he would wear the ordinary gun cases, she knew she could make them so well that no one would suspect the sex of the tailor.

But by this time, Mr Barton has finished his pipe, the candle begins to burn low, and Mrs Barton goes to see if Nanny has succeeded in lulling Walter to sleep. Nanny is that moment putting him in the little cot by his mother's bedside; the head, with its thin wavelets of brown hair, indents the little pillow, and a tiny, waxen, dimpled fist hides the rosy lips, for baby is given to the infantile peccadillo of thumb-sucking. So Nanny could now join in the short evening prayer, and all could go to bed.

Mrs Barton carried upstairs the remainder of her heap of stockings, and laid them on a table close to her bedside, where also she placed a warm shawl, removing her candle, before she put it out, to a tin socket fixed at the head of her bed. Her body was very weary, but her heart was not heavy, in spite of Mr Woods the butcher, and the transitory nature of shoe leather, for her heart so overflowed with love, she felt sure she was near a fountain of love that would care for husband and babes better than she could foresee; so she was soon asleep. But about half-past five in the morning, if there were any angels watching round her bed – and angels might be glad of such an office – they saw Mrs Barton rise up quietly, careful not to disturb the slumbering Amos, who was snoring the snore of the just, light her candle, prop herself upright with the pillows, throw the warm shawl round her shoulders, and renew her attack on the heap of undarned stockings. She darned away until she heard Nanny stirring, and then drowsiness came with the dawn, the candle was put out, and she sank into a doze. But at nine o'clock she was at the breakfast table, busy cutting bread and butter for five hungry mouths, while Nanny, baby on one arm, in rosy cheeks, fat neck, and nightgown, brought in a jug of hot milk and water. Nearest her mother sits the nine-year-old Patty, the eldest child, whose sweet fair face is already rather grave sometimes, and who always wants to run upstairs to save mamma's legs, which get so tired of an evening. Then there are four other blond heads – two boys and two girls, gradually decreasing in size down to Chubby, who is making a round O of her mouth to receive a bit of Papa's 'baton'. Papa's attention was divided between petting Chubby, rebuking the noisy Fred, which he did with a somewhat excessive sharpness, and eating his own breakfast. He had not yet looked at Mamma, and did not know that her cheek was paler than usual. But Patty whispered, 'Mamma, have you the headache?'

Happily coal was cheap in the neighbourhood of Shepperton, and Mr Hackit would any time let his horses draw a load for 'the parson' without charge, so there was a blazing fire in the sitting-room, and not without need, for the vicarage garden, as they looked out on it from the bow-window, was hard with black frost, and the sky had the white woolly look that portends snow.

Breakfast over, Mr Barton mounted to his study, and occupied himself in the first place with his letter to Mr Oldinport. It was very much the same sort of letter as most clergymen would have written under the same circumstances, except that instead of 'perambulate', the Revd Amos wrote 'preambulate', and instead of 'if haply', 'if happily', the contingency indicated being the reverse of happy. Mr Barton had not the gift of perfect accuracy in English orthography and syntax, which was unfortunate, as he was known not to be a Hebrew scholar, and not in the least suspected of being an accomplished Grecian. These lapses, in a man who had gone through the Eleusinian mysteries[10] of a university education, surprised the young ladies of his parish extremely – especially the Misses Farquhar, whom he had once addressed in a letter as Dear Mads., apparently an abbreviation for Madams. The persons least surprised at the Revd Amos' deficiencies were his clerical brethren, who had gone through the mysteries themselves. At eleven o'clock, Mr Barton walked forth in cape and boa, with the sleet driving in his face, to read prayers at the workhouse, euphemistically called the 'College'. The College was a huge square stone building, standing on the best apology for an elevation of ground that could be seen for about ten miles around Shepperton. A flat ugly district this, depressing enough to look at even on the brightest days. The roads are black with coal dust, the brick houses dingy with smoke, and at that time – the time of handloom weavers – every other cottage had a loom at its window, where you might see a pale, sickly-looking man or woman pressing a narrow chest against a board, and doing a sort of treadmill work with legs and arms. A troublesome district for a clergyman – at least to one who, like Amos Barton, understood the 'cure of souls' in something more than an official sense; for over and above the rustic stupidity furnished by the farm labourers, the miners brought obstreperous animalism, and the weavers an acrid Radicalism and Dissent. Indeed, Mrs Hackit often observed that the colliers, who many of them earned better wages than Mr Barton, 'passed their time in doing nothing but swilling ale and smoking, like the beasts that perish' (speaking, we may presume, in a remotely analogical sense); and in some of the alehouse corners the drink was flavoured by a dingy kind of infidelity, something like rinsings of Tom Paine[11] in ditch-water. A certain amount of religious excitement created by the popular preaching of Mr Parry, Amos' predecessor, had nearly died out, and the religious life of Shepperton was falling back towards low water mark. Here, you perceive, was a terrible stronghold of Satan, and you may well pity the Revd Amos Barton, who had to stand single-handed and summon it to surrender. We read, indeed, that the walls of Jericho fell down before the sound of trumpets, but we nowhere hear that those trumpets were hoarse and feeble. Doubtless they were

26

trumpets that gave forth clear ringing tones, and sent a mighty vibration through brick and mortar. But the oratory of the Revd Amos resembled rather a Belgian railway-horn, which shows praiseworthy intentions inadequately fulfilled. He often missed the right note both in public and private exhortation, and got a little angry in consequence. For though Amos thought himself strong, he did not *feel* himself strong. Nature had given him the opinion, but not the sensation. Without that opinion he would probably never have worn cambric bands, but would have been an excellent cabinet-maker and deacon of an Independent church, as his father was before him (he was not a shoemaker, as Mr Pilgrim had reported). He might then have sniffed long and loud in the corner of his pew in Gun Street Chapel; he might have indulged in halting rhetoric at prayer-meetings, and have spoken faulty English in private life; and these little infirmities would not have prevented him – honest, faithful man that he was – from being a shining light in the Dissenting circle of Bridgeport. A tallow dip, of the long-eight description, is an excellent thing in the kitchen candlestick, and Betty's nose and eye are not sensitive to the difference between it and the finest wax; it is only when you stick it in the silver candlestick, and introduce it into the drawing-room, that it seems plebeian, dim, and ineffectual. Alas for the worthy man who, like that candle, gets himself into the wrong place! It is only the very largest souls who will be able to appreciate and pity him – who will discern and love sincerity of purpose amid all the bungling feebleness of achievement.

But now Amos Barton has made his way through the sleet as far as the College, has thrown off his hat, cape, and boa, and is reading, in the dreary stone-floored dining-room, a portion of the morning service to the inmates seated on the benches before him. Remember, the New Poor Law[12] had not yet come into operation, and Mr Barton was not acting as paid chaplain of the Union, but as the pastor who had the cure of all souls in his parish, pauper as well as other. After the prayers, he always addressed to them a short discourse on some subject suggested by the lesson for the day, striving if by this means some edifying matter might find its way into the pauper mind and conscience – perhaps a task as trying as you could well imagine to the faith and patience of any honest clergyman. For, on the very first bench, these were the faces on which his eye had to rest, watching whether there was any stirring under the stagnant surface. Right in front of him – probably because he was stone deaf, and it was deemed more edifying to hear nothing at a short distance than at a long one – sat 'Old Maxum', as he was familiarly called, his real patronymic remaining a mystery to most persons. A fine philological sense discerns in this cognomen an indication that the pauper patriarch had once been considered pithy and sententious in his speech, but now the weight of ninety-five years lay heavy on his tongue as well as in his ears, and he sat before the clergyman with protruded chin, and munching mouth, and eyes that seemed to look at emptiness.

Next to him sat Poll Fodge – known to the magistracy of her county as Mary Higgins – a one-eyed woman, with a scarred and seamy face, the most notorious rebel in the workhouse, said to have once thrown her broth over the master's coat-tails, and who, in spite of Nature's apparent safeguards against that contingency, had contributed to the perpetuation of the Fodge characteristics in the person of a small boy, who was behaving naughtily on one of the back benches. Miss Fodge fixed her one sore eye on Mr Barton with a sort of hardy defiance.

Beyond this member of the softer sex, at the end of the bench, sat 'Silly Jim', a young man afflicted with hydrocephalus, who rolled his head from side to side, and gazed at the point of his nose. These were the supporters of Old Maxum on his right.

On his left sat Mr Fitchett, a tall fellow, who had once been a footman in the Oldinport family, and in that giddy elevation had enunciated a contemptuous opinion of boiled beef, which had been traditionally handed down in Shepperton as the direct cause of his ultimate reduction to pauper commons. His calves were now shrunken, and his hair was grey without the aid of powder, but he still carried his chin as if he were conscious of a stiff cravat; he set his dilapidated hat on with a knowing inclination towards the left ear; and when he was on fieldwork, he carted and uncarted the manure with a sort of flunkey grace, the ghost of that jaunty demeanour with which he used to usher in my lady's morning visitors. The flunkey nature was nowhere completely subdued but in his stomach, and he still divided society into gentry, gentry's flunkeys, and the people who provided for them. A clergyman without a flunkey was an anomaly, belonging to neither of these classes. Mr Fitchett had an irrepressible tendency to drowsiness under spiritual instruction, and in the recurrent regularity with which he dozed off until he nodded and woke himself, he looked not unlike a piece of mechanism, ingeniously contrived for measuring the length of Mr Barton's discourse.

Perfectly wide awake, on the contrary, was his left-hand neighbour, Mrs Brick, one of those hard undying old women to whom age seems to have given a network of wrinkles, as a coat of magic armour against the attacks of winters, warm or cold. The point on which Mrs Brick was still sensitive – the theme on which you might possibly excite her hope and fear –

was snuff. It seemed to be an embalming powder, helping her soul to do the office of salt.

And now, eke out an audience of which this front benchful was a sample, with a certain number of refractory children, over whom Mr Spratt, the master of the workhouse, exercised an irate surveillance, and I think you will admit that the university-taught clergyman, whose office it is to bring home the gospel to a handful of such souls, has a sufficiently hard task. For, to have any chance of success, short of miraculous intervention, he must bring his geographical, chronological, exegetical mind pretty nearly to the pauper point of view, or of no view; he must have some approximate conception of the mode in which the doctrines that have so much vitality in the plenum of his own brain will comport themselves *in vacuo*, that is to say, in a brain that is neither geographical, chronological, nor exegetical. It is a flexible imagination that can take such a leap as that, and an adroit tongue that can adapt its speech to so unfamiliar a position. The Revd Amos Barton had neither that flexible imagination, nor that adroit tongue. He talked of Israel and its sins, of chosen vessels, of the Paschal Lamb, of blood as a medium of reconciliation; and he strove in this way to convey religious truth within reach of the Fodge and Fitchett mind. This very morning, the first lesson was the twelfth chapter of Exodus, and Mr Barton's exposition turned on unleavened bread. Nothing in the world more suited to the simple understanding than instruction through familiar types and symbols! But there is always this danger attending it, that the interest or comprehension of your hearers may stop short precisely at the point where your spiritual interpretation begins. And Mr Barton this morning succeeded in carrying the pauper imagination to the dough-tub, but unfortunately was not able to carry it upwards from that well-known object to the unknown truths which it was intended to shadow forth.

Alas! a natural incapacity for teaching, finished by keeping 'terms' at Cambridge, where there are able mathematicians, and butter is sold by the yard, is not apparently the medium through which Christian doctrine will distil as welcome dew on withered souls.

And so, while the sleet outside was turning to unquestionable snow, and the stony dining-room looked darker and drearier, and Mr Fitchett was nodding his lowest, and Mr Spratt was boxing the boys' ears with a constant rinforzando, as he felt more keenly the approach of dinner-time, Mr Barton wound up his exhortation with something of the February chill at his heart as well as his feet. Mr Fitchett, thoroughly roused now the instruction was at an end, obsequiously and gracefully advanced to help Mr Barton in putting on his cape, while Mrs Brick rubbed her withered forefinger round and round her little shoe-shaped snuffbox, vainly seeking for the fraction of a pinch. I can't help thinking that if Mr Barton had shaken into that little box a small portion of Scotch high-dried, he might have produced something more like an amiable emotion in Mrs Brick's mind than anything she had felt under his morning's exposition of the unleavened bread. But our good Amos laboured under a deficiency of small tact as well as of small cash; and when he observed the action of the old woman's forefinger, he said, in his brusque way, 'So your snuff is all gone, eh?' Mrs Brick's eyes twinkled with the visionary hope that the parson might be intending to replenish her box, at least mediately, through the present of a small copper.

'Ah, well! you'll soon be going where there is no more snuff. You'll be in need of mercy then. You must remember that you may have to seek for mercy and not find it, just as you're seeking for snuff.'

At the first sentence of this admonition, the twinkle subsided from Mrs Brick's eyes. The lid of her box went 'click!' and her heart was shut up at the same moment.

But now Mr Barton's attention was called for by Mr Spratt, who was dragging a small and unwilling boy from the rear. Mr Spratt was a small-featured, small-statured man with a remarkable power of language, mitigated by hesitation, who piqued himself on expressing unexceptionable sentiments in unexceptional language on all occasions.

'Mr Barton, sir – aw – aw – excuse my trespassing on your time – aw – to beg that you will administer a rebuke to this boy; he is – aw – aw – most inveterate in ill-behaviour during service-time.'

The inveterate culprit was a boy of seven, vainly contending against 'candles' at his nose by feeble sniffing. But no sooner had Mr Spratt uttered his impeachment than Miss Fodge rushed forward and placed herself between Mr Barton and the accused.

'That's *my* child, Muster Barton,' she exclaimed, further manifesting her maternal instincts by applying her apron to her offspring's nose. 'He's al'ys a-findin' fault wi' him, and a-poundin' him for nothin'. Let him goo an' eat his roost goose as is a-smellin' up in our noses while we're a-swallering them greasy broth, an' let my boy alooan.' Mr Spratt's small eyes flashed, and he was in danger of uttering sentiments not unexceptionable before the clergyman. But Mr Barton, foreseeing that a prolongation of this episode would not be to edification, said 'Silence!' in his severest tones. 'Let me hear no abuse. Your boy is not likely to behave well if you set him the example of being saucy.' Then stooping down to Master Fodge, and taking him by the shoulder, 'Do you like being beaten?'

'No-a.'

'Then what a silly boy you are to be naughty. If you were not naughty, you wouldn't be beaten. But if you are naughty, God will be angry, as well as Mr Spratt, and God can burn you for ever. That will be worse than being beaten.'

Master Fodge's countenance was neither affirmative nor negative of this proposition.

'But,' continued Mr Barton, 'if you will be a good boy, God will love you, and you will grow up to be a good man. Now, let me hear next Thursday that you have been a good boy.'

Master Fodge had no distinct vision of the benefit that would accrue to him from this change of courses. But Mr Barton, being aware that Miss Fodge had touched on a delicate subject in alluding to the roast goose, was determined to witness no more polemics between her and Mr Spratt, so, saying good morning to the latter, he hastily left the College.

The snow was falling in thicker and thicker flakes, and already the vicarage garden was cloaked in white as he passed through the gate. Mrs Barton heard him open the door, and ran out of the sitting-room to meet him.

'I'm afraid your feet are very wet, dear. What a terrible morning! Let me take your hat. Your slippers are at the fire.'

Mr Barton was feeling a little cold and cross. It is difficult, when you have been doing disagreeable duties, without praise, on a snowy day, to attend to the very minor morals. So he showed no recognition of Milly's attentions, but simply said, 'Fetch me my dressing-gown, will you?'

'It *is* down, dear. I thought you wouldn't go into the study because you said you would letter and number the books for the Lending Library. Patty and I have been covering them, and they are all ready in the sitting-room.'

'Oh, I can't do those this morning,' said Mr Barton, as he took off his boots and put his feet into the slippers Milly had brought him, 'you must put them away into the parlour.'

The sitting-room was also the day nursery and schoolroom, and while Mamma's back was turned, Dickey, the second boy, had insisted on superseding Chubby in the guidance of a headless horse, of the red-wafered species, which she was drawing round the room, so that when Papa opened the door Chubby was giving tongue energetically.

'Milly, some of these children must go away. I want to be quiet.'

'Yes, dear. Hush, Chubby; go with Patty, and see what Nanny is getting for our dinner. Now, Fred and Sophy and Dickey, help me to carry these books into the parlour. There are three for Dickey. Carry them steadily.'

Papa meanwhile settled himself in his easy chair, and took up a work on Episcopacy, which he had from the Clerical Book Society, thinking he would finish it and return it this afternoon as he was going to the Clerical Meeting at Milby Vicarage where the Book Society had its headquarters. The Clerical Meetings and Book Society, which had been founded some eight or ten months, had had a noticeable effect on the Revd Amos Barton. When he first came to Shepperton he was simply an evangelical clergyman whose Christian experiences had commenced under the teaching of the Revd Mr Johns, of Gun Street Chapel, and had been consolidated at Cambridge under the influence of Mr Simeon. John Newton and Thomas Scott were his doctrinal ideals; he would have taken in the *Christian Observer* and the *Record*, if he could have afforded it; his anecdotes were chiefly of the pious-jocose kind, current in Dissenting circles, and he thought an Episcopalian Establishment unobjectionable.[13]

But, by this time, the effect of the Tractarian agitation[14] was beginning to be felt in backward provincial regions, and the Tractarian satire on the Low-Church party was beginning to tell even on those who disavowed or resisted Tractarian doctrines. The vibration of an intellectual movement was felt from the golden head to the miry toes of the Establishment; and so it came to pass that, in the district round Milby, the market town close to Shepperton, the clergy had agreed to have a clerical meeting every month, wherein they would exercise their intellects by discussing theological and ecclesiastical questions, and cement their brotherly love by discussing a good dinner. A Book Society naturally suggested itself as an adjunct of this agreeable plan, and thus, you perceive, there was provision made for ample friction of the clerical mind.

Now, the Revd Amos Barton was one of those men who have a decided will and opinion of their own; he held himself bolt upright, and had no self-distrust. He would march very determinedly along the road he thought best, but then it was wonderfully easy to convince him which *was* the best road. And so a very little unwonted reading and unwonted discussion made him see that an Episcopalian Establishment was much more than unobjectionable, and on many other points he began to feel that he held opinions a little too far-sighted and profound to be crudely and suddenly communicated to ordinary minds. He was like an onion that has been rubbed with spices – the strong original odour was blended with something new and foreign. The Low-Church onion still offended refined High-Church nostrils, and the new spice was unwelcome to the palate of the genuine onion-eater.

We will not accompany him to the Clerical Meeting today,

because we shall probably want to go thither some day when he will be absent. And just now I am bent on introducing you to Mr Bridmain and the Countess Czerlaski, with whom Mr and Mrs Barton are invited to dine tomorrow.

3

Outside, the moon is shedding its cold light on the cold snow, and the white-bearded fir trees round Camp Villa are casting a blue shadow across the white ground, while the Revd Amos Barton and his wife are audibly crushing the crisp snow beneath their feet, as, about seven o'clock on Friday evening, they approach the door of the above-named desirable country residence, containing dining-, breakfast-, and drawing-rooms, etc., situated only half a mile from the market town of Milby.

Inside, there is a bright fire in the drawing-room, casting a pleasant but uncertain light on the delicate silk dress of a lady who is reclining behind a screen in the corner of the sofa, and allowing you to discern that the hair of the gentleman who is seated in the armchair opposite, with a newspaper over his knees, is becoming decidedly grey. A little 'King Charles', with a crimson ribbon round his neck, who has been lying curled up in the very middle of the hearthrug, has just discovered that that zone is too hot for him, and is jumping on the sofa, evidently with the intention of accommodating his person on the silk gown. On the table there are two wax candles, which will be lit as soon as the expected knock is heard at the door. The knock is heard, the candles are lit, and presently Mr and Mrs Barton are ushered in – Mr Barton, erect and clerical, in a faultless tie and shining cranium; Mrs Barton graceful in a newly turned black silk.

'Now this is charming of you,' said the Countess Czerlaski, advancing to meet them, and embracing Milly with careful elegance. 'I am really ashamed of my selfishness in asking my friends to come and see me in this frightful weather.' Then, giving her hand to Amos: 'And you, Mr Barton, whose time is so precious! But I am doing a good deed in drawing you away from your labours. I have a plot to prevent you from martyrising yourself.'

While this greeting was going forward, Mr Bridmain, and Jet the spaniel, looked on with the air of actors who had no idea of byplay. Mr Bridmain, a stiff and rather thick-set man, gave his welcome with a laboured cordiality. It was astonishing how very little he resembled his beautiful sister. For the Countess Czerlaski was undeniably beautiful. As she seated herself by Mrs Barton on the sofa, Milly's eyes, indeed, rested – must it be confessed? – chiefly on the details of the tasteful dress, the rich silk of a pinkish lilac hue (the Countess always wore delicate colours in an evening), the black lace pelerine, and the black lace veil falling at the back of the small, closely braided head. For Milly had one weakness – don't love her any the less for it, it was a pretty woman's weakness – she was fond of dress, and often, when she was making up her own economical millinery, she had romantic visions how nice it would be to put on really handsome stylish things – to have very stiff balloon sleeves, for example, without which a woman's dress was nought in those days. You and I, too, reader, have our weakness, have we not? which makes us think foolish things now and then. Perhaps it may lie in an excessive admiration for small hands and feet, a tall lithe figure, large dark eyes, and dark silken braided hair. All these the Countess possessed, and she had, moreover, a delicately formed nose, the least bit curved, and a clear brunette complexion. Her mouth, it must be admitted, receded too much from her nose and chin, and to a prophetic eye threatened 'nutcrackers' in advanced age. But by the light of fire and wax candles, that age seemed very far off indeed, and you would have said that the Countess was not more than thirty.

Look at the two women on the sofa together! The large, fair, mild-eyed Milly is timid even in friendship: it is not easy to her to speak of the affection of which her heart is full. The lithe, dark, thin-lipped Countess is racking her small brain for caressing words and charming exaggerations.

'And how are all the cherubs at home?' said the Countess, stooping to pick up Jet, and without waiting for an answer: 'I have been kept indoors by a cold ever since Sunday or I should not have rested without seeing you. What have you done with those wretched singers, Mr Barton?'

'Oh, we have got a new choir together, which will go on very well with a little practice. I was quite determined that the old set of singers should be dismissed. I had given orders that they should not sing the wedding psalm, as they call it, again, to make a new-married couple look ridiculous, and they sang it in defiance of me. I could put them into the Ecclesiastical Court if I chose for to do so, for lifting up their voices in church in opposition to the clergyman.'

'And a most wholesome discipline that would be,' said the Countess. 'Indeed, you are too patient and forbearing, Mr Barton. For my part, *I* lose *my* temper when I see how far you are from being appreciated in that miserable Shepperton.'

If, as is probable, Mr Barton felt at a loss what to say in reply to the insinuated compliment, it was a relief to him that dinner was announced just then, and that he had to offer his arm to the Countess.

As Mr Bridmain was leading Mrs Barton to the dining-room, he observed, 'The weather is very severe.'

'Very, indeed,' said Milly.

Mr Bridmain studied conversation as an art. To ladies he spoke of the weather, and was accustomed to consider it under three points of view: as a question of climate in general, comparing England with other countries in this respect; as a personal question, enquiring how it affected his lady inter-locutor in particular; and as a question of probabilities, discussing whether there would be a change or a continuance of the present atmospheric conditions. To gentlemen he talked politics, and he read two daily papers expressly to qualify himself for this function. Mr Barton thought him a man of considerable political information, but not of lively parts.

'And so you are always to hold your Clerical Meetings at Mr Ely's?' said the Countess, between her spoonfuls of soup. (The soup was a little over-spiced. Mrs Short of Camp Villa, who was in the habit of letting her best apartments, gave only moderate wages to her cook.)

'Yes,' said Mr Barton, 'Milby is a central place, and there are many conveniences in having only one point of meeting.'

'Well,' continued the Countess, 'everyone seems to agree in giving the precedence to Mr Ely. For my part, I *cannot* admire him. His preaching is too cold for me. It has no fervour – no heart. I often say to my brother it is a great comfort to me that Shepperton Church is not too far off for us to go to, don't I, Edmund?'

'Yes,' answered Mr Bridmain, 'they show us into such a bad pew at Milby – just where there is a draught from that door. I caught a stiff neck the first time I went there.'

'Oh, it is the cold in the pulpit that affects me, not the cold in the pew. I was writing to my friend Lady Porter this morning, and telling her all about my feelings. She and I think alike on such matters. She is most anxious that when Sir William has an opportunity of giving away the living at their place, Dippley, they should have a thoroughly zealous clever man there. I have been describing a certain friend of mine to her, who, I think, would be just to her mind. And there is such a pretty rectory, Milly. Shouldn't I like to see you the mistress of it?'

Milly smiled and blushed slightly. The Revd Amos blushed very red, and gave a little embarrassed laugh – he could rarely keep his muscles within the limits of a smile.

At this moment John, the manservant, approached Mrs Barton with a gravy tureen, and also with a slight odour of the stable, which usually adhered to him through his indoor functions. John was rather nervous, and the Countess, happening to speak to him at this inopportune moment, the tureen slipped and emptied itself on Mrs Barton's newly turned black silk.

'Oh, horror! Tell Alice to come directly and rub Mrs Barton's dress,' said the Countess to the trembling John, carefully abstaining from approaching the gravy-sprinkled spot on the floor with her own lilac silk. But Mr Bridmain, who had a strictly private interest in silks, good-naturedly jumped up and applied his napkin at once to Mrs Barton's gown. Milly felt a little inward anguish, but no ill-temper, and tried to make light of the matter for the sake of John as well as others. The Countess felt inwardly thankful that her own delicate silk had escaped, but threw out lavish interjections of distress and indignation.

'Dear saint that you are,' she said, when Milly laughed and suggested that, as her silk was not very glossy to begin with, the dim patch would not be much seen; 'you don't mind about these things, I know. Just the same sort of thing happened to me at the Princess Wengstein's one day, on a pink satin. I was in an agony. But you are so indifferent to dress, and well you may be. It is you who make dress pretty, and not dress that makes you pretty.'

Alice, the buxom lady's maid, wearing a much better dress than Mrs Barton's, now appeared to take Mr Bridmain's place in retrieving the mischief, and after a great amount of supplementary rubbing, composure was restored, and the business of dining was continued.

When John was recounting his accident to the cook in the kitchen, he observed, 'Mrs Barton's a hamable woman. I'd a deal sooner ha' throwed the gravy o'er the Countess' fine gownd. But laws! what tantrums she'd ha' been in arter the visitors was gone.'

'You'd a deal sooner not ha' throwed it down at all, *I* should think,' responded the unsympathetic cook, to whom John did *not* make love. 'Who d'you think's to make gravy anuff, if you're to baste people's gownds wi' it?'

'Well,' suggested John, humbly, 'you should wet the bottom of the duree a bit, to hold it from slippin'.'

'Wet your granny!' returned the cook, a retort which she probably regarded in the light of a *reductio ad absurdum*, and which in fact reduced John to silence. Later on in the evening, while John was removing the tea-things from the drawing-room, and brushing the crumbs from the tablecloth with an accompanying hiss, such as he was wont to encourage himself with in rubbing down Mr Bridmain's horse, the Revd Amos Barton drew from his pocket a thin green-covered pamphlet, and, presenting it to the Countess, said, 'You were pleased, I think, with my sermon on Christmas Day. It has been printed in *The Pulpit*, and I thought you might like a copy.'

'That indeed I shall. I shall quite value the opportunity of reading that sermon. There was such depth in it! – such argument! It was not a sermon to be heard only once. I am delighted that it should become generally known, as it will be now it is printed in *The Pulpit*.'

'Yes,' said Milly, innocently, 'I was so pleased with the editor's letter.' And she drew out her little pocketbook where she carefully treasured the editorial autograph, while Mr Barton laughed and blushed, and said, 'Nonsense, Milly!'

'You see,' she said, giving the letter to the Countess, 'I am very proud of the praise my husband gets.' The sermon in question, by the by, was an extremely argumentative one on the Incarnation, which, as it was preached to a congregation not one of whom had any doubt of that doctrine, and to whom the Socinians therein confuted were as unknown as the Arimaspians, was exceedingly well adapted to trouble and confuse the Sheppertonian mind.[15]

'Ah,' said the Countess, returning the editor's letter, 'he may well say he will be glad of other sermons from the same source. But I would rather you should publish your sermons in an independent volume, Mr Barton. It would be so desirable to have them in that shape. For instance, I could send a copy to the Dean of Radborough. And there is Lord Blarney, whom I knew before he was chancellor. I was a special favourite of his, and you can't think what sweet things he used to say to me. I shall not resist the temptation to write to him one of these days *sans façon*, and tell him how he ought to dispose of the next vacant living in his gift.'

Whether Jet the spaniel, being a much more knowing dog than was suspected, wished to express his disapproval of the Countess' last speech as not accordant with his ideas of wisdom and veracity, I cannot say, but at this moment he jumped off her lap, and, turning his back upon her, placed one paw on the fender, and held the other up to warm, as if affecting to abstract himself from the current of conversation.

But now Mr Bridmain brought out the chessboard, and Mr Barton accepted his challenge to play a game, with immense satisfaction. The Revd Amos was very fond of chess, as most people are who can continue through many years to create interesting vicissitudes in the game by taking long-meditated moves with their knights, and subsequently discovering that they have thereby exposed their queen.

Chess is a silent game, and the Countess' chat with Milly is in quite an undertone – probably relating to women's matters that it would be impertinent for us to listen to; so we will leave Camp Villa, and proceed to Milby Vicarage, where Mr Farquhar has sat out two other guests with whom he has been dining at Mr Ely's, and is now rather wearying that reverend gentleman by his protracted small-talk.

Mr Ely was a tall, dark-haired, distinguished-looking man of three and thirty. By the laity of Milby and its neighbourhood he was regarded as a man of quite remarkable powers and learning, who must make a considerable sensation in London pulpits and drawing-rooms on his occasional visit to the metropolis; and by his brother clergy he was regarded as a discreet and agreeable fellow. Mr Ely never got into a warm discussion; he suggested what might be thought, but rarely said what he thought himself. He never let either men or women see that he was laughing at them, and he never gave anyone an opportunity of laughing at *him*. In one thing only he was injudicious. He parted his dark wavy hair down the middle, and as his head was rather flat than otherwise, that style of coiffure was not advantageous to him.

Mr Farquhar, though not a parishioner of Mr Ely's, was

one of his warmest admirers, and thought he would make an unexceptionable son-in-law, in spite of his being of no particular 'family'. Mr Farquhar was susceptible on the point of 'blood' – his own circulating fluid, which animated a short and somewhat flabby person, being, he considered, of very superior quality.

'By the by,' he said, with a certain pomposity counteracted by a lisp, 'what an ath Barton makth of himthelf, about that Bridmain and the Counteth, ath she callth herthelf. After you were gone the other evening, Mithith Farquhar wath telling him the general opinion about them in the neighbourhood, and he got quite red and angry. Bleth your thoul, he believth the whole thtory about her Polish huthband and hith wonderful ethcapeth; and ath for her – why, he thinkth her perfection, a woman of motht refined fellingth, and no end of thtuff.'

Mr Ely smiled. 'Some people would say our friend Barton was not the best judge of refinement. Perhaps the lady flatters him a little, and we men are susceptible. She goes to Shepperton Church every Sunday – drawn there, let us suppose, by Mr Barton's eloquence.'

'Pthaw,' said Mr Farquhar. 'Now, to my mind, you have only to look at that woman to thee what she ith – throwing her eyth about when she comth into church, and drething in a way to attract attention. I should thay, she'th tired of her brother Bridmain, and looking out for another brother with a thtronger family likeneth. Mithith Farquhar ith very fond of Mithith Barton, and ith quite dithtrethed that she should athothiate with thuch a woman, tho she attacked him on the thubject purpothly. But I tell her it'th of no uthe, with a pig-headed fellow like him. Barton'th well-meaning enough, but *tho* contheited. I've left off giving him my advithe.'

Mr Ely smiled inwardly and said to himself, 'What a punishment!' But to Mr Farquhar he said, 'Barton might be more judicious, it must be confessed.' He was getting tired, and did not want to develop the subject.

'Why, nobody vithit-th them but the Bartonth,' continued Mr Farquhar, 'and why should thuch people come here, unleth they had particular reathonth for preferring a neighbourhood where they are not known? Pooh! it lookth bad on the very fathe of it. *You* called on them, now; how did you find them?'

'Oh, Mr Bridmain strikes me as a common sort of man, who is making an effort to seem wise and well bred. He comes down on one tremendously with political information, and seems knowing about the King of the French. The Countess is certainly a handsome woman, but she puts on the grand air a little too powerfully. Woodcock was immensely taken with her, and insisted on his wife's calling on her and asking her to dinner, but I think Mrs Woodcock turned restive after the first visit, and wouldn't invite her again.'

'Ha, ha! Woodcock hath alwayth a thoft place in hith heart for a pretty fathe. It'th odd how he came to marry that plain woman, and no fortune either.'

'Mysteries of the tender passion,' said Mr Ely. 'I am not initiated yet, you know.'

Here Mr Farquhar's carriage was announced, and as we have not found his conversation particularly brilliant under the stimulus of Mr Ely's exceptional presence, we will not accompany him home to the less exciting atmosphere of domestic life. Mr Ely threw himself with a sense of relief into his easiest chair, set his feet on the hobs, and in this attitude of bachelor enjoyment began to read Bishop Jebb's memoirs[16].

I am by no means sure that if the good people of Milby had known the truth about the Countess Czerlaski, they would not have been considerably disappointed to find that it was very far from being as bad as they imagined. Nice distinctions are troublesome. It is so much easier to say that a thing is black than to discriminate the particular shade of brown, blue, or green, to which it really belongs. It is so much easier to make up your mind that your neighbour is good for nothing, than to enter into all the circumstances that would oblige you to modify that opinion.

Besides, think of all the virtuous declamation, all the penetrating observation, which had been built up entirely on the fundamental position that the Countess was a very objectionable person indeed, and which would be utterly overturned and nullified by the destruction of that premiss. Mrs Phipps, the banker's wife, and Mrs Landor, the attorney's wife, had invested part of their reputation for acuteness in the supposition that Mr Bridmain was not the Countess' brother. Moreover, Miss Phipps was conscious that if the Countess was not a disreputable person, she, Miss Phipps, had no compensating superiority in virtue to set against the other lady's manifest superiority in personal charms. Miss Phipps' stumpy figure and unsuccessful attire, instead of looking down from a mount of virtue with an aureole round its head, would then be seen on the same level and in the same light as the Countess Czerlaski's Diana-like form and well-chosen drapery. Miss Phipps, for her part, didn't like dressing for effect – she had always avoided that style of appearance which was calculated to create a sensation.

Then what amusing innuendoes of the Milby gentlemen

over their wine would have been entirely frustrated and reduced to nought, if you had told them that the Countess had really been guilty of no misdemeanours which demanded her exclusion from strictly respectable society; that her husband had been the veritable Count Czerlaski, who had had wonderful escapes, as she said, and who, as she did *not* say, but as was said in certain circulars once folded by her fair hands, had subsequently given dancing lessons in the metropolis; that Mr Bridmain was neither more nor less than her half-brother, who, by unimpeached integrity and industry, had won a partnership in a silk-manufactory, and thereby a moderate fortune that enabled him to retire, as you see, to study politics, the weather, and the art of conversation at his leisure. Mr Bridmain, in fact, quadragenarian bachelor as he was, felt extremely well pleased to receive his sister in her widowhood, and to shine in the reflected light of her beauty and title. Every man who is not a monster, a mathematician, or a mad philosopher, is the slave of some woman or other. Mr Bridmain had put his neck under the yoke of his handsome sister, and though his soul was a very little one – of the smallest description indeed – he would not have ventured to call it his own. He might be slightly recalcitrant now and then, as is the habit of long-eared pachyderms, under the thong of the fair Countess' tongue, but there seemed little probability that he would ever get his neck loose. Still, a bachelor's heart is an outlying fortress that some fair enemy may any day take either by storm or stratagem, and there was always the possibility that Mr Bridmain's first nuptials might occur before the Countess was quite sure of her second. As it was, however, he submitted to all his sister's caprices, never grumbled because her dress and her maid formed a considerable item beyond her own little income of sixty pounds per annum, and consented to lead with her a migratory life, as personages on the debatable ground between aristocracy and commonalty, instead of settling in some spot where his five hundred a year might have won him the definite dignity of a parochial magnate.

The Countess had her views in choosing a quiet provincial place like Milby. After three years of widowhood, she had brought her feelings to contemplate giving a successor to her lamented Czerlaski, whose fine whiskers, fine air, and romantic fortunes had won her heart ten years ago, when, as pretty Caroline Bridmain, in the full bloom of five and twenty, she was governess to Lady Porter's daughters, whom he initiated into the mysteries of the *pas de basque* and the Lancers' quadrilles. She had had seven years of sufficiently happy matrimony with Czerlaski, who had taken her to Paris and Germany, and introduced her there to many of his old friends with large titles and small fortunes. So that the fair Caroline had had considerable experience of life, and had gathered therefrom, not, indeed, any very ripe and comprehensive wisdom, but much external polish, and certain practical conclusions of a very decided kind. One of these conclusions was that there were things more solid in life than fine whiskers and a title, and that, in accepting a second husband, she would regard these items as quite subordinate to a carriage and a settlement. Now, she had ascertained, by tentative residences, that the kind of bite she was angling for was difficult to be met with at watering places, which were already preoccupied with an abundance of angling beauties, and were chiefly stocked with men whose whiskers might be dyed, and whose incomes were still more problematic; so she had determined on trying a neighbourhood where people were extremely well acquainted with each other's affairs, and where the women were mostly ill dressed and ugly. Mr Bridmain's slow brain had adopted his sister's views, and it seemed to him that a woman so handsome and distinguished as the Countess must certainly make a match that might lift himself into the region of county celebrities, and give him at least a sort of cousinship to the quarter sessions.

All this, which was the simple truth, would have seemed extremely flat to the gossips of Milby, who had made up their minds to something much more exciting. There was nothing here so very detestable. It is true, the Countess was a little vain, a little ambitious, a little selfish, a little shallow and frivolous, a little given to white lies. But who considers such slight blemishes, such moral pimples as these, disqualifications for entering into the most respectable society! Indeed, the severest ladies in Milby would have been perfectly aware that these characteristics would have created no wide distinction between the Countess Czerlaski and themselves; and since it was clear there was a wide distinction – why, it must lie in the possession of some vices from which they were undeniably free.

Hence it came to pass that Milby respectability refused to recognise the Countess Czerlaski, in spite of her assiduous churchgoing and the deep disgust she was known to have expressed at the extreme paucity of the congregations on Ash Wednesdays. So she began to feel that she had miscalculated the advantages of a neighbourhood where people are well acquainted with each other's private affairs. Under these circumstances, you will imagine how welcome was the perfect credence and admiration she met with from Mr and Mrs Barton. She had been especially irritated by Mr Ely's behaviour to her; she felt sure that he was not in the least struck with her beauty, that he quizzed her conversation, and that he spoke of her with a sneer. A woman always knows where she is utterly powerless, and shuns a coldly satirical eye as she would shun a Gorgon. And she was especially eager for clerical notice and friendship, not merely because that is quite the most respectable countenance to be obtained in society, but because she really cared about religious matters, and had an uneasy sense that she was not altogether safe in that quarter. She had serious intentions of becoming *quite* pious – without any reserves – when she had once got her carriage and settlement. Let us do this one sly trick, says Ulysses to Neoptolemus, and we will be perfectly honest ever after:

> *all' hedu gar toi ktema tes nikes labein,*
> *tolma: dikaioi d'authis ekphanoumetha.*[17]

The Countess did not quote Sophocles, but she said to herself, 'Only this little bit of pretence and vanity, and then I will be *quite* good, and make myself quite safe for another world.'

And as she had by no means such fine taste and insight in theological teaching as in costume, the Revd Amos Barton seemed to her a man not only of learning – *that* is always understood with a clergyman – but of as much power as a spiritual director. As for Milly, the Countess really loved her as well as the preoccupied state of her affections would allow. For you have already perceived that there was one being to whom the Countess was absorbingly devoted, and to whose desires she made everything else subservient – namely, Caroline Czerlaski, née Bridmain.

Thus there was really not much affectation in her sweet speeches and attentions to Mr and Mrs Barton. Still their friendship by no means adequately represented the object she had in view when she came to Milby, and it had been for some time clear to her that she must suggest a new change of residence to her brother.

The thing we look forward to often comes to pass, but never precisely in the way we have imagined to ourselves. The Countess did actually leave Camp Villa before many months were past, but under circumstances which had not at all entered into her contemplation.

5

The Revd Amos Barton, whose sad fortunes I have undertaken to relate, was, you perceive, in no respect an ideal or exceptional character, and perhaps I am doing a bold thing to bespeak your sympathy on behalf of a man who was so very far from remarkable – a man whose virtues were not heroic, and who had no undetected crime within his breast; who had not the slightest mystery hanging about him, but was palpably and unmistakably commonplace; who was not even in love, but had had that complaint favourably many years ago. 'An utterly uninteresting character!' I think I hear a lady reader exclaim – Mrs Farthingale, for example, who prefers the ideal in fiction; to whom tragedy means ermine tippets, adultery and murder; and comedy, the adventures of some personage who is quite a 'character'.

But, my dear madam, it is so very large a majority of your fellow-countrymen that are of this insignificant stamp. At least eighty out of a hundred of your adult male fellow-Britons returned in the last census are neither extraordinarily silly, nor extraordinarily wicked, nor extraordinarily wise. Their eyes are neither deep and liquid with sentiment, nor sparkling with suppressed witticisms; they have probably had no hairbreadth escapes or thrilling adventures; their brains are certainly not pregnant with genius, and their passions have not manifested themselves at all after the fashion of a volcano. They are simply men of complexions more or less muddy, whose conversation is more or less bald and disjointed. Yet these commonplace people – many of them – bear a conscience, and have felt the sublime prompting to do the painful right; they have their unspoken sorrows, and their sacred joys; their hearts have perhaps gone out towards their first-born, and they have mourned over the irreclaimable dead. Nay, is there not a pathos in their very insignificance – in our comparison of their dim and narrow existence with the glorious possibilities of that human nature which they share?

Depend upon it, you would gain unspeakably if you would learn with me to see some of the poetry and the pathos, the tragedy and the comedy, lying in the experience of a human soul that looks out through dull grey eyes, and that speaks in a voice of quite ordinary tones. In that case, I should have no fear of your not caring to know what further befell the Revd Amos Barton, or of your thinking the homely details I have to tell at all beneath your attention. As it is, you can, if you please, decline to pursue my story further; and you will easily find reading more to your taste, since I learn from the newspapers that many remarkable novels, full of striking situations, thrilling incidents, and eloquent writing, have appeared only within the last season.

Meanwhile, readers who have begun to feel an interest in the Revd Amos Barton and his wife, will be glad to learn that Mr Oldinport lent the twenty pounds. But twenty pounds are soon exhausted when twelve are due as back payment to the butcher, and when the possession of eight extra sovereigns in February weather is an irresistible temptation to order a new greatcoat. And though Mr Bridmain so far departed from the necessary economy entailed on him by the Countess' elegant toilette and expensive maid, as to choose a handsome black silk, stiff – as his experienced eye discerned – with the genuine strength of its own texture, and not with the factitious strength of gum, and present it to Mrs Barton, in retrieval of the accident that had occurred at his table, yet, dear me – as every husband has heard – what is the present of a gown when you are deficiently furnished with the etceteras of apparel, and when, moreover, there are six children whose wear and tear of clothes is something incredible to the non-maternal mind?

Indeed, the equation of income and expenditure was offering new and constantly accumulating difficulties to Mr and Mrs Barton; for shortly after the birth of little Walter, Milly's aunt, who had lived with her ever since her marriage, had withdrawn herself, her furniture, and her yearly income, to the household of another niece; prompted to that step, very probably, by a slight 'tiff' with the Revd Amos, which occurred while Milly was upstairs, and proved one too many for the elderly lady's patience and magnanimity. Mr Barton's temper was a little warm, but, on the other hand, elderly maiden ladies are known to be susceptible, so we will not suppose that all the blame lay on his side – the less so, as he had every motive for humouring an inmate whose presence kept the wolf from the door. It was now nearly a year since Miss Jackson's departure, and, to a fine ear, the howl of the wolf was audibly approaching.

It was a sad thing, too, that when the last snow had melted, when the purple and yellow crocuses were coming up in the garden, and the old church was already half pulled down, Milly had an illness which made her lips look pale, and rendered it absolutely necessary that she should not exert herself for some time. Mr Brand, the Shepperton doctor so obnoxious to

Mr Pilgrim, ordered her to drink port-wine, and it was quite necessary to have a charwoman very often to assist Nanny in all the extra work that fell upon her.

Mrs Hackit, who hardly ever paid a visit to anyone but her oldest and nearest neighbour, Mrs Patten, now took the unusual step of calling at the vicarage one morning; and the tears came into her unsentimental eyes as she saw Milly seated pale and feeble in the parlour, unable to persevere in sewing the pinafore that lay on the table beside her. Little Dickey, a boisterous boy of five, with large pink cheeks and sturdy legs, was having his turn to sit with Mamma, and was squatting quiet as a mouse at her knee, holding her soft white hand between his little red black-nailed fists. He was a boy whom Mrs Hackit, in a severe mood, had pronounced 'stocky' (a word that etymologically, in all probability, conveys some allusion to an instrument of punishment for the refractory); but seeing him thus subdued into goodness, she smiled at him with her kindest smile, and stooping down, suggested a kiss – a favour which Dickey resolutely declined.

'Now *do* you take nourishing things enough?' was one of Mrs Hackit's first questions, and Milly endeavoured to make it appear that no woman was ever so much in danger of being overfed and led into self-indulgent habits as herself. But Mrs Hackit gathered one fact from her replies, namely, that Mr Brand had ordered port-wine.

While this conversation was going forward, Dickey had been furtively stroking and kissing the soft white hand; so that at last, when a pause came, his mother said, smilingly, 'Why are you kissing my hand, Dickey?'

'It id *to* yovely,' answered Dickey, who, you observe, was decidedly backward in his pronunciation.

Mrs Hackit remembered this little scene in after-days, and

thought with peculiar tenderness and pity of the 'stocky boy'.

The next day there came a hamper with Mrs Hackit's respects, and on being opened it was found to contain half a dozen of port-wine and two couples of fowls. Mrs Farquhar, too, was very kind; insisted on Mrs Barton's rejecting all arrowroot but hers, which was genuine Indian, and carried away Sophy and Fred to stay with her a fortnight. These and other good-natured attentions made the trouble of Milly's illness more bearable; but they could not prevent it from swelling expenses, and Mr Barton began to have serious thoughts of representing his case to a certain charity for the relief of needy curates.

Altogether, as matters stood in Shepperton, the parishioners were more likely to have a strong sense that the clergyman needed their material aid than that they needed his spiritual aid – not the best state of things in this age and country, where faith in men solely on the ground of their spiritual gifts has considerably diminished, and especially unfavourable to the influence of the Revd Amos, whose spiritual gifts would not have had a very commanding power even in an age of faith.

But, you ask, did not the Countess Czerlaski pay any attention to her friends all this time? To be sure she did. She was indefatigable in visiting her 'sweet Milly', and sitting with her for hours together. It may seem remarkable to you that she neither thought of taking away any of the children, nor of providing for any of Milly's probable wants, but ladies of rank and of luxurious habits, you know, cannot be expected to surmise the details of poverty. She put a great deal of eau de Cologne on Mrs Barton's pocket handkerchief, rearranged her pillow and footstool, kissed her cheeks, wrapped her in a soft warm shawl from her own shoulders, and amused her with stories of the life she had seen abroad. When Mr Barton joined them she talked of Tractarianism, of her determination not to re-enter the vortex of fashionable life, and of her anxiety to see him in a sphere large enough for his talents. Milly thought her sprightliness and affectionate warmth quite charming, and was very fond of her; while the Revd Amos had a vague consciousness that he had risen into aristocratic life, and only associated with his middle-class parishioners in a pastoral and parenthetic manner.

However, as the days brightened, Milly's cheeks and lips brightened too; and in a few weeks she was almost as active as ever, though watchful eyes might have seen that activity was not easy to her. Mrs Hackit's eyes were of that kind, and one day, when Mr and Mrs Barton had been dining with her for the first time since Milly's illness, she observed to her husband: 'That poor thing's dreadful weak an' dilicate; she won't stan' havin' many more children.'

Mr Barton, meanwhile, had been indefatigable in his vocation. He had preached two extemporary sermons every Sunday at the workhouse, where a room had been fitted up for divine service, pending the alterations in the church; and had walked the same evening to a cottage at one or other extremity of his parish to deliver another sermon, still more extemporary, in an atmosphere impregnated with spring flowers and perspiration. After all these labours you will easily conceive that he was considerably exhausted by half-past nine in the evening, and that a supper at a friendly parishioner's, with a glass, or even two glasses, of brandy and water after it, was a welcome reinforcement. Mr Barton was not at all an ascetic; he thought the benefits of fasting were entirely confined to the Old Testament dispensation; he was fond of relaxing himself with a little gossip; indeed, Miss Bond, and other ladies of enthusiastic views, sometimes regretted that Mr Barton did not more uninterruptedly exhibit a superiority to the things of the flesh. Thin ladies, who take little exercise, and whose livers are not strong enough to bear stimulants, are so extremely critical about one's personal habits! And, after all, the Revd Amos never came near the borders of a vice. His very faults were middling – he was not *very* ungrammatical. It was not in his nature to be superlative in anything; unless, indeed, he was superlatively middling, the quintessential extract of mediocrity. If there was any one point on which he showed an inclination to be excessive, it was confidence in his own shrewdness and ability in practical matters, so that he was very full of plans which were something like his moves in chess – admirably well calculated, supposing the state of the case were otherwise. For example, that notable plan of introducing anti-Dissenting books into his Lending Library did not in the least appear to have bruised the head of Dissent, though it had certainly made Dissent strongly inclined to bite the Revd Amos' heel. Again, he vexed the souls of his churchwardens and influential parishioners by his fertile suggestiveness as to what it would be well for them to do in the matter of the church repairs, and other ecclesiastical secularities.

'I never saw the like to parsons,' Mr Hackit said one day in conversation with his brother churchwarden, Mr Bond. 'They're al'ys for meddling with business, an they know no more about it than my black filly.'

'Ah,' said Mr Bond, 'they're too high-learnt to have much common sense.'

'Well,' remarked Mr Hackit, in a modest and dubious tone, as if throwing out a hypothesis which might be considered bold, 'I should say that's a bad sort of eddication as makes folks unreasonable.'

So that, you perceive, Mr Barton's popularity was in that precarious condition, in that toppling and contingent state in which a very slight push from a malignant destiny would utterly upset it. That push was not long in being given, as you shall hear.

One fine May morning, when Amos was out on his parochial visits, and the sunlight was streaming through the bow-window of the sitting-room, where Milly was seated at her sewing, occasionally looking up to glance at the children playing in the garden, there came a loud rap at the door, which she at once recognised as the Countess', and that well-dressed lady presently entered the sitting-room, with her veil drawn over her face. Milly was not at all surprised or sorry to see her; but when the Countess threw up her veil, and showed that her eyes were red and swollen, she was both surprised and sorry.

'What can be the matter, dear Caroline?'

Caroline threw down Jet, who gave a little yelp; then she threw her arms round Milly's neck, and began to sob; then she threw herself on the sofa, and begged for a glass of water; then she threw off her bonnet and shawl; and by the time Milly's imagination had exhausted itself in conjuring up calamities, she said: 'Dear, how shall I tell you? I am the most wretched woman. To be deceived by a brother to whom I have been so devoted – to see him degrading himself – giving himself utterly to the dogs!'

'What can it be?' said Milly, who began to picture to herself the sober Mr Bridmain taking to brandy and betting.

'He is going to be married – to marry my own maid, that deceitful Alice, to whom I have been the most indulgent mistress. Did you ever hear of anything so disgraceful? so mortifying? so disreputable?'

'And has he only just told you of it?' said Milly, who,

having really heard of worse conduct, even in her innocent life, avoided a direct answer.

'Told me of it! He had not even the grace to do that. I went into the dining-room suddenly and found him kissing her – disgusting at his time of life, is it not? – and when I reproved her for allowing such liberties, she turned round saucily and said she was engaged to be married to my brother, and she saw no shame in allowing him to kiss her. Edmund is a miserable coward, you know, and looked frightened; but when she asked him to say whether it was not so, he tried to summon up courage and say yes. I left the room in disgust, and this morning I have been questioning Edmund, and find that he is bent on marrying this woman, and that he has been putting off telling me – because he was ashamed of himself, I suppose. I couldn't possibly stay in the house after this, with my own maid turned mistress. And now, Milly, I am come to throw myself on your charity for a week or two. *Will* you take me in?'

'That we will,' said Milly, 'if you will only put up with our poor rooms and way of living. It will be delightful to have you!'

'It will soothe me to be with you and Mr Barton a little while. I feel quite unable to go among my other friends just at present. What those two wretched people will do I don't know – leave the neighbourhood at once, I hope. I entreated my brother to do so, before he disgraced himself.'

When Amos came home, he joined his cordial welcome and sympathy to Milly's. By and by the Countess' formidable boxes, which she had carefully packed before her indignation drove her away from Camp Villa, arrived at the vicarage, and were deposited in the spare bedroom, and in two closets, not spare, which Milly emptied for their reception. A week afterwards, the excellent apartments at Camp Villa, comprising dining- and drawing-rooms, three bedrooms and a dressing-room, were again to let, and Mr Bridmain's sudden departure, together with the Countess Czerlaski's installation as a visitor at Shepperton Vicarage, became a topic of general conversation in the neighbourhood. The keen-sighted virtue of Milby and Shepperton saw in all this a confirmation of its worst suspicions, and pitied the Revd Amos Barton's gullibility.

But when week after week, and month after month, slipped by without witnessing the Countess' departure – when summer and harvest had fled, and still left her behind them occupying the spare bedroom and the closets, and also a large proportion of Mrs Barton's time and attention, new surmises of a very evil kind were added to the old rumours, and began to take the form of settled convictions in the minds even of Mr Barton's most friendly parishioners.

And now, here is an opportunity for an accomplished writer to apostrophise calumny, to quote Virgil[18], and to show that he is acquainted with the most ingenious things which have been said on that subject in polite literature.

But what is opportunity to the man who can't use it? An unfecundated egg, which the waves of time wash away into nonentity. So, as my memory is ill furnished, and my notebook still worse, I am unable to show myself either erudite or eloquent apropos of the calumny whereof the Revd Amos Barton was the victim. I can only ask my reader: did you ever upset your ink bottle, and watch, in helpless agony, the rapid spread of Stygian blackness over your fair manuscript or fairer table cover? With a like inky swiftness did gossip now blacken the reputation of the Revd Amos Barton, causing the unfriendly to scorn and even the friendly to stand aloof, at a time when difficulties of another kind were fast thickening around him.

6

One November morning, at least six months after the Countess Czerlaski had taken up her residence at the vicarage, Mrs Hackit heard that her neighbour, Mrs Patten, had an attack of her old complaint, vaguely called 'the spasms'. Accordingly, about eleven o'clock, she put on her velvet bonnet and cloth cloak, with a long boa and muff large enough to stow a prize baby in; for Mrs Hackit regulated her costume by the calendar, and brought out her furs on the first of November, whatever might be the temperature. She was not a woman weakly to accommodate herself to shilly-shally proceedings. If the season didn't know what it ought to do, Mrs Hackit did. In her best days, it was always sharp weather at 'Gunpowder Plot', and she didn't like new fashions.

And this morning the weather was very rationally in accordance with her costume, for as she made her way through the fields to Cross Farm, the yellow leaves on the hedge-girt elms, which showed bright and golden against the long-hanging purple clouds, were being scattered across the grassy path by the coldest of November winds. 'Ah,' Mrs Hackit thought to herself, 'I dare say we shall have a sharp pinch this winter, and if we do, I shouldn't wonder if it takes the old lady off. They say a green Yule makes a fat churchyard, but so does a white Yule too, for that matter. When the stool's rotten enough, no matter who sits on it.'

However, on her arrival at Cross Farm, the prospect of Mrs Patten's decease was again thrown into the dim distance in her imagination, for Miss Janet Gibbs met her with the news that Mrs Patten was much better, and led her, without any preliminary announcement, to the old lady's bedroom. Janet had scarcely reached the end of her circumstantial narrative how the attack came on and what were her aunt's sensations – a narrative to which Mrs Patten, in her neatly plaited nightcap, seemed to listen with a contemptuous resignation to her niece's historical inaccuracy, contenting herself with occasionally confounding Janet by a shake of the head – when the clatter of a horse's hoofs on the yard pavement announced the arrival of Mr Pilgrim, whose large, top-booted person presently made its appearance upstairs. He found Mrs Patten going on so well that there was no need to look solemn. He might glide from condolence into gossip without offence, and the temptation of having Mrs Hackit's ear was irresistible.

'What a disgraceful business this is turning out of your parson's,' was the remark with which he made this agreeable transition, throwing himself back in the chair from which he had been leaning towards the patient.

'Eh, dear me!' said Mrs Hackit, 'disgraceful enough. I stuck to Mr Barton as long as I could, for his wife's sake, but I can't countenance such goings-on. It's hateful to see that woman coming with 'em to service of a Sunday, and if Mr Hackit wasn't churchwarden and I didn't think it wrong to forsake one's own parish, I should go to Knebley Church. There's a many parish'ners as do.'

'I used to think Barton was only a fool,' observed Mr Pilgrim, in a tone which implied that he was conscious of having been weakly charitable. 'I thought he was imposed upon and led away by those people when they first came. But that's impossible now.'

'Oh, it's as plain as the nose in your face,' said Mrs Hackit, unreflectingly, not perceiving the equivoque in her comparison – 'comin' to Milby, like a sparrow perchin' on a bough, as I may say, with her brother, as she called him; and then all on a sudden the brother goes off with himself, and she throws

62

herself on the Bartons. Though what could make her take up with a poor notomise[19] of a parson, as hasn't got enough to keep wife and children, there's One above knows – *I* don't.'

'Mr Barton may have attractions we don't know of,' said Mr Pilgrim, who piqued himself on a talent for sarcasm. 'The Countess has no maid now, and they say Mr Barton is handy in assisting at her toilette – laces her boots, and so forth.'

'Tilette, be fiddled!' said Mrs Hackit, with indignant boldness of metaphor. 'An there's that poor thing a-sewing her fingers to the bone for them children – an' another comin' on. What she must have to go through! It goes to my heart to turn my back on her. But she's i' the wrong to let herself be put upon i' that manner.'

'Ah! I was talking to Mrs Farquhar about that the other day. She said, "I think Mrs Barton a v-e-r-y w-e-a-k w-o-m-a-n."' (Mr Pilgrim gave this quotation with slow emphasis, as if he thought Mrs Farquhar had uttered a remarkable sentiment.) 'They find it impossible to invite her to their house while she has that equivocal person staying with her.'

'Well!' remarked Miss Gibbs, 'if I was a wife, nothing should induce me to bear what Mrs Barton does.'

'Yes, it's fine talking,' said Mrs Patten, from her pillow; 'old maids' husbands are al'ys well managed. If you was a wife you'd be as foolish as your betters, belike.'

'All my wonder is,' observed Mrs Hackit, 'how the Bartons make both ends meet. You may depend on it, *she*'s got nothing to give 'em; for I understand as he's been having money from some clergy charity. They said at fust as she stuffed Mr Barton wi' notions about her writing to the Chancellor an' her fine friends, to give him a living. Howiver, I don't know what's true an' what's false. Mr Barton keeps away from our house now, for I gave him a bit o' my mind one day. Maybe he's

63

ashamed of himself. He seems to me to look dreadful thin an' harassed of a Sunday.'

'Oh, he must be aware he's getting into bad odour everywhere. The clergy are quite disgusted with his folly. They say Carpe would be glad to get Barton out of the curacy if he could; but he can't do that without coming to Shepperton himself, as Barton's a licensed curate, and he wouldn't like that, I suppose.'

At this moment Mrs Patten showed signs of uneasiness, which recalled Mr Pilgrim to professional attentions; and Mrs Hackit, observing that it was Thursday, and she must see after the butter, said goodbye, promising to look in again soon, and bring her knitting.

This Thursday, by the by, is the first in the month – the day on which the Clerical Meeting is held at Milby Vicarage; and as the Revd Amos Barton has reasons for not attending, he will very likely be a subject of conversation amongst his clerical brethren. Suppose we go there, and hear whether Mr Pilgrim has reported their opinion correctly.

There is not a numerous party today, for it is a season of sore throats and catarrhs; so that the exegetical and theological discussions, which are the preliminary of dining, have not been quite so spirited as usual; and although a question relative to the Epistle of Jude has not been quite cleared up, the striking of six by the church clock, and the simultaneous announcement of dinner, are sounds that no one feels to be importunate.

Pleasant (when one is not in the least bilious) to enter a comfortable dining-room, where the closely drawn red curtains glow with the double light of fire and candle, where glass and silver are glittering on the pure damask, and a soup tureen gives a hint of the fragrance that will presently rush out to inundate your hungry senses, and prepare them, by the delicate visitation of atoms, for the keen gusto of ampler contact! Especially if you have confidence in the dinner-giving capacity of your host – if you know that he is not a man who entertains grovelling views of eating and drinking as a mere satisfaction of hunger and thirst, and, dead to all the finer influences of the palate, expects his guest to be brilliant on ill-flavoured gravies and the cheapest Marsala. Mr Ely was particularly worthy of such confidence, and his virtues as an Amphitryon[20] had probably contributed quite as much as the central situation of Milby to the selection of his house as a clerical rendezvous. He looks particularly graceful at the head of his table, and, indeed, on all occasions where he acts as president or moderator, he is a man who seems to listen well, and is an excellent amalgam of dissimilar ingredients.

At the other end of the table, as 'Vice', sits Mr Fellowes, rector and magistrate, a man of imposing appearance, with a mellifluous voice and the readiest of tongues. Mr Fellowes once obtained a living by the persuasive charms of his conversation, and the fluency with which he interpreted the opinions of an obese and stammering baronet, so as to give that elderly gentleman a very pleasing perception of his own wisdom. Mr Fellowes is a very successful man, and has the highest character everywhere except in his own parish, where, doubtless because his parishioners happen to be quarrelsome people, he is always at fierce feud with a farmer or two, a colliery proprietor, a grocer who was once churchwarden, and a tailor who formerly officiated as clerk.

At Mr Ely's right hand you see a very small man with a sallow and somewhat puffy face, whose hair is brushed straight up, evidently with the intention of giving him a height somewhat less disproportionate to his sense of his own importance than the measure of five feet three accorded him by an oversight of Nature. This is Revd Archibald Duke, a very dyspeptic and evangelical man, who takes the gloomiest view of mankind and their prospects, and thinks the immense sale of the *Pickwick Papers*, recently completed, one of the strongest proofs of original sin. Unfortunately, though Mr Duke was not burdened with a family, his yearly expenditure was apt considerably to exceed his income; and the unpleasant circumstances resulting from this, together with heavy meat-breakfasts, may probably have contributed to his desponding views of the world generally.

Next to him is seated Mr Furness, a tall young man, with blond hair and whiskers, who was plucked at Cambridge[21] entirely owing to his genius; at least I know that he soon after-wards published a volume of poems, which were considered remarkably beautiful by many young ladies of his acquaintance. Mr Furness preached his own sermons, as anyone of tolerable critical acumen might have certified by comparing them with his poems: in both, there was an exuberance of metaphor and simile entirely original, and not in the least borrowed from any resemblance in the things compared.

On Mr Furness' left you see Mr Pugh, another young curate, of much less marked characteristics. He had not published any poems; he had not even been plucked; he had neat black whiskers and a pale complexion, read prayers and a sermon twice every Sunday, and might be seen any day sallying forth on his parochial duties in a white tie, a well-brushed hat, a perfect suit of black, and well-polished boots – an equipment which he probably supposed hieroglyphically to represent the spirit of Christianity to the parishioners of Whittlecombe.

Mr Pugh's vis-à-vis is the Revd Martin Cleves, a man about

forty – middle-sized, broad-shouldered, with a negligently tied cravat, large irregular features, and a large head, thickly covered with lanky brown hair. To a superficial glance, Mr Cleves is the plainest and least clerical-looking of the party; yet, strange to say, there is the true parish priest, the pastor beloved, consulted, relied on by his flock; a clergyman who is not associated with the undertaker, but thought of as the surest helper under a difficulty, as a monitor who is encouraging rather than severe. Mr Cleves has the wonderful art of preaching sermons which the wheelwright and the blacksmith can understand – not because he talks condescending twaddle, but because he can call a spade a spade, and knows how to disencumber ideas of their wordy frippery. Look at him more attentively, and you will see that his face is a very interesting one – that there is a great deal of humour and feeling playing in his grey eyes, and about the corners of his roughly cut mouth: a man, you observe, who has most likely sprung from the harder-working section of the middle class, and has hereditary sympathies with the chequered life of the people. He gets together the working men in his parish on a Monday evening, and gives them a sort of conversational lecture on useful practical matters, telling them stories, or reading some select passages from an agreeable book, and commenting on them; and if you were to ask the first labourer or artisan in Tripplegate what sort of man the parson was, he would say, 'a uncommon knowin', sensable, free-spoken gentleman; very kind an' good-natur'd too'. Yet for all this, he is perhaps the best Grecian of the party, if we except Mr Baird, the young man on his left.

Mr Baird has since gained considerable celebrity as an original writer and metropolitan lecturer, but at that time he used to preach in a little church something like a barn, to a congregation consisting of three rich farmers and their servants, about fifteen labourers, and the due proportion of women and children. The rich farmers understood him to be 'very high-learnt'; but if you had interrogated them for a more precise description, they would have said that he was 'a thinnish-faced man, with a sort o' cast in his eye, like'.

Seven, altogether: a delightful number for a dinner party, supposing the units to be delightful, but everything depends on that. During dinner Mr Fellowes took the lead in the conversation, which set strongly in the direction of mangel-wurzel and the rotation of crops, for Mr Fellowes and Mr Cleves cultivated their own glebes[22]. Mr Ely, too, had some agricultural notions, and even the Revd Archibald Duke was made alive to that class of mundane subjects by the possession of some potato-ground. The two young curates talked a little aside during these discussions, which had imperfect interest for their unbeneficed minds; and the transcendental and near-sighted Mr Baird seemed to listen somewhat abstractedly, knowing little more of potatoes and mangel-wurzel than that they were some form of the 'Conditioned'.

'What a hobby farming is with Lord Watling!' said Mr Fellowes, when the cloth was being drawn. 'I went over his farm at Tetterley with him last summer. It is really a model farm: first-rate dairy, grazing and wheat land, and such splendid farm buildings! An expensive hobby, though. He sinks a good deal of money there, I fancy. He has a great whim for black cattle, and he sends that drunken old Scotch bailiff of his to Scotland every year, with hundreds in his pocket, to buy these beasts.'

'By the by,' said Mr Ely, 'do you know who is the man to whom Lord Watling has given the Bramhill living?'

'A man named Sargent. I knew him at Oxford. His brother

is a lawyer, and was very useful to Lord Watling in that ugly Brounsell affair. That's why Sargent got the living.'

'Sargent,' said Mr Ely. 'I know him. Isn't he a showy, talkative fellow; has written travels in Mesopotamia, or something of that sort?'

'That's the man.'

'He was at Witherington once, as Bagshawe's curate. He got into rather bad odour there through some scandal about a flirtation, I think.'

'Talking of scandal,' returned Mr Fellowes, 'have you heard the last story about Barton? Nisbett was telling me the other day that he dines alone with the Countess at six, while Mrs Barton is in the kitchen acting as cook.'

'Rather an apocryphal authority, Nisbett,' said Mr Ely.

'Ah,' said Mr Cleves, with good-natured humour twinkling in his eyes, 'depend upon it, that is a corrupt version. The original text is that they all dined together *with* six – meaning six children – and that Mrs Barton is an excellent cook.'

'I wish dining alone together may be the worst of that sad business,' said the Revd Archibald Duke, in a tone implying that his wish was a strong figure of speech.

'Well,' said Mr Fellowes, filling his glass and looking jocose, 'Barton is certainly either the greatest gull in existence, or he has some cunning secret – some philtre or other to make himself charming in the eyes of a fair lady. It isn't all of us that can make conquests when our ugliness is past its bloom.'

'The lady seemed to have made a conquest of him at the very outset,' said Mr Ely. 'I was immensely amused one night at Granby's when he was telling us her story about her husband's adventures. He said, "When she told me the tale, I felt I don't know how – I felt it from the crown of my head to the sole of my feet."'

Mr Ely gave these words dramatically, imitating the Revd Amos' fervour and symbolic action, and everyone laughed except Mr Duke, whose after-dinner view of things was not apt to be jovial. He said, 'I think some of us ought to remonstrate with Mr Barton on the scandal he is causing. He is not only imperilling his own soul, but the souls of his flock.'

'Depend upon it,' said Mr Cleves, 'there is some simple explanation of the whole affair, if we only happened to know it. Barton has always impressed me as a right-minded man who has the knack of doing himself injustice by his manner.'

'Now *I* never liked Barton,' said Mr Fellowes. 'He's not a gentleman. Why, he used to be on terms of intimacy with that canting Prior, who died a little while ago – a fellow who soaked himself with spirits, and talked of the gospel through an inflamed nose.'

'The Countess has given him more refined tastes, I dare say,' said Mr Ely.

'Well,' observed Mr Cleves, 'the poor fellow must have a hard pull to get along, with his small income and large family. Let us hope the Countess does something towards making the pot boil.'

'Not she,' said Mr Duke. 'There are greater signs of poverty about them than ever.'

'Well, come,' returned Mr Cleves, who could be caustic sometimes, and who was not at all fond of his reverend brother, Mr Duke, 'that's something in Barton's favour at all events. He might be poor *without* showing signs of poverty.'

Mr Duke turned rather yellow, which was his way of blushing, and Mr Ely came to his relief by observing, 'They're making a very good piece of work of Shepperton Church. Dolby, the architect, who has it in hand, is a very clever fellow.'

'It's he who has been doing Coppleton Church,' said

Mr Furness. 'They've got it in excellent order for the visitation.'

This mention of the visitation suggested the Bishop, and thus opened a wide duct, which entirely diverted the stream of animadversion from that small pipe – that capillary vessel, the Revd Amos Barton.

The talk of the clergy about their Bishop belongs to the esoteric part of their profession, so we will at once quit the dining-room at Milby Vicarage lest we should happen to overhear remarks unsuited to the lay understanding, and perhaps dangerous to our repose of mind.

7

I dare say the long residence of the Countess Czerlaski at Shepperton Vicarage is very puzzling to you also, dear reader, as well as to Mr Barton's clerical brethren; the more so, as I hope you are not in the least inclined to put that very evil interpretation on it which evidently found acceptance with the sallow and dyspeptic Mr Duke, and with the florid and highly peptic Mr Fellowes. You have seen enough, I trust, of the Revd Amos Barton to be convinced that he was more apt to fall into a blunder than into a sin – more apt to be deceived than to incur a necessity for being deceitful, and if you have a keen eye for physiognomy, you will have detected that the Countess Czerlaski loved herself far too well to get entangled in an unprofitable vice.

How then, you will say, could this fine lady choose to quarter herself on the establishment of a poor curate where the carpets were probably falling into holes, where the attendance was limited to a maid-of-all-work, and where six children were running loose from eight o'clock in the morning till eight o'clock in the evening? Surely you must be straining probability.

Heaven forbid! For not having a lofty imagination, as you perceive, and being unable to invent thrilling incidents for your amusement, my only merit must lie in the truth with which I represent to you the humble experience of ordinary fellow-mortals. I wish to stir your sympathy with common-place troubles – to win your tears for real sorrow: sorrow such as may live next door to you – such as walks neither in rags nor in velvet, but in very ordinary decent apparel.

Therefore, that you may dismiss your suspicions as to the truth of my picture, I will beg you to consider that at the time the Countess Czerlaski left Camp Villa in dudgeon, she had only twenty pounds in her pocket, being about one third of the income she possessed independently of her brother. You will then perceive that she was in the extremely inconvenient predicament of having quarrelled, not indeed with her bread and cheese, but certainly with her chicken and tart – a predicament all the more inconvenient to her, because the habit of idleness had quite unfitted her for earning those necessary superfluities, and because, with all her fascinations, she had not secured any enthusiastic friends whose houses were open to her, and who were dying to see her. Thus she had completely checkmated herself, unless she could resolve on one unpleasant move – namely, to humble herself to her brother, and recognise his wife. This seemed quite impossible to her as long as she entertained the hope that he would make the first advances; and in this flattering hope she remained month after month at Shepperton Vicarage, gracefully over-looking the deficiencies of accommodation, and feeling that she was really behaving charmingly. 'Who indeed,' she thought to herself, 'could do otherwise, with a lovely, gentle creature like Milly? I shall really be sorry to leave the poor thing.'

So, though she lay in bed till ten, and came down to a separate breakfast at eleven, she kindly consented to dine as early as five, when a hot joint was prepared, which coldly furnished forth the children's table the next day; she considerately prevented Milly from devoting herself too closely to the children, by insisting on reading, talking, and walking with her; and she even began to embroider a cap for the next baby, which must certainly be a girl, and be named Caroline.

After the first month or two of her residence at the vicarage, the Revd Amos Barton became aware – as, indeed, it was unavoidable that he should – of the strong disapprobation it drew upon him, and the change of feeling towards him which it was producing in his kindest parishioners. But, in the first place, he still believed in the Countess as a charming and influential woman, disposed to befriend him, and, in any case, he could hardly hint departure to a lady guest who had been kind to him and his, and who might any day spontaneously announce the termination of her visit; in the second place, he was conscious of his own innocence, and felt some contemptuous indignation towards people who were ready to imagine evil of him; and, lastly, he had, as I have already intimated, a strong will of his own, so that a certain obstinacy and defiance mingled itself with his other feelings on the subject.

The one unpleasant consequence which was not to be evaded or counteracted by any mere mental state, was the increasing drain on his slender purse for household expenses, to meet which the remittance he had received from the clerical charity threatened to be quite inadequate. Slander may be defeated by equanimity; but courageous thoughts will not pay your baker's bill, and fortitude is nowhere considered legal tender for beef. Month after month, the financial aspect of the Revd Amos' affairs became more and more serious to him, and month after month, too, wore away more and more of that armour of indignation and defiance with which he had at first defended himself from the harsh looks of faces that were once the friendliest.

But quite the heaviest pressure of the trouble fell on Milly – on gentle, uncomplaining Milly – whose delicate body was becoming daily less fit for all the many things that had to be done between rising up and lying down. At first, she thought the Countess' visit would not last long, and she was quite glad to incur extra exertion for the sake of making her friend comfortable. I can hardly bear to think of all the rough work she did with those lovely hands – all by the sly, without letting her husband know anything about it, and husbands are not clairvoyant: how she salted bacon, ironed shirts and cravats, put patches on patches, and redarned darns. Then there was the task of mending and eking out baby-linen in prospect, and the problem perpetually suggesting itself how she and Nanny *should* manage when there was another baby, as there would be before very many months were past.

When time glided on, and the Countess' visit did not end, Milly was not blind to any phase of their position. She knew of the slander; she was aware of the keeping aloof of old friends, but these she felt almost entirely on her husband's account. A loving woman's world lies within the four walls of her own home, and it is only through her husband that she is in any electric communication with the world beyond. Mrs Simpkins may have looked scornfully at her, but baby crows and holds out his little arms none the less blithely; Mrs Tomkins may have left off calling on her, but her husband comes home none the less to receive her care and caresses; it has been wet and gloomy out of doors today, but she has looked well after the shirt buttons, has cut out baby's pinafores, and half finished Willy's blouse.

So it was with Milly. She was only vexed that her husband should be vexed – only wounded because he was mis-conceived. But the difficulty about ways and means she felt in quite a different manner. Her rectitude was alarmed lest they should have to make tradesmen wait for their money; her motherly love dreaded the diminution of comforts for the children; and the sense of her own failing health gave exaggerated force to these fears.

Milly could no longer shut her eyes to the fact that the Countess was inconsiderate, if she did not allow herself to entertain severer thoughts; and she began to feel that it would soon be a duty to tell her frankly that they really could not afford to have her visit further prolonged. But a process was going forward in two other minds, which ultimately saved Milly from having to perform this painful task.

In the first place, the Countess was getting weary of Shepperton – weary of waiting for her brother's overtures which never came. So, one fine morning, she reflected that forgiveness was a Christian duty, that a sister should be placable, that Mr Bridmain must feel the need of her advice, to which he had been accustomed for three years, and that very likely 'that woman' didn't make the poor man happy. In this amiable frame of mind she wrote a very affectionate appeal, and addressed it to Mr Bridmain, through his banker.

Another mind that was being wrought up to a climax was Nanny's, the maid-of-all-work, who had a warm heart and a still warmer temper. Nanny adored her mistress: she had been heard to say that she was 'ready to kiss the ground as the missis trod on'; and Walter, she considered, was *her* baby, of whom she was as jealous as a lover. But she had, from the first, very slight admiration for the Countess Czerlaski. That lady, from Nanny's point of view, was a personage always 'drawed out i' fine clothes', the chief result of whose existence was to cause additional bedmaking, carrying of hot water, laying of tablecloths, and cooking of dinners. It was a perpetually heightening 'aggravation' to Nanny that she and her mistress had to 'slave' more than ever, because there was this fine lady in the house.

'An, she pays nothin' for't neither,' observed Nanny to Mr Jacob Tomms, a young gentleman in the tailoring line, who occasionally – simply out of a taste for dialogue – looked into the vicarage kitchen of an evening. 'I know the master's shorter o' money than iver, an' it meks no end o' difference i' th' housekeepin' her bein' here, besides bein' obliged to have a charwoman constant.'

'There's fine stories i' the village about her,' said Mr Tomms. 'They say as Muster Barton's great wi' her, or else she'd niver stop here.'

'Then they say a passill o' lies, an' you ought to be ashamed to go an' tell 'em o'er again. Do you think as the master, as has got a wife like the missis, 'ud go running arter a stuck-up piece o' goods like that Countess as isn't fit to black the missis' shoes? I'm none so fond o' the master, but I know better on him nor that.'

'Well, I didn't b'lieve it,' said Mr Tomms, humbly.

'B'lieve it? you'd ha' been a ninny if yer did. An' she's a nasty, stingy thing, that Countess. She's niver giv me a sixpence nor an old rag neither, sin' here's she's been. A-lyin' a bed an a-comin' down to breakfast when other folks wants their dinner!'

If such was the state of Nanny's mind as early as the end of August, when this dialogue with Mr Tomms occurred, you may imagine what it must have been by the beginning of November, and that at that time a very slight spark might any day cause the long-smouldering anger to flame forth in open indignation.

That spark happened to fall the very morning that Mrs Hackit paid the visit to Mrs Patten, recorded in the last chapter. Nanny's dislike of the Countess extended to the innocent dog Jet, whom she 'couldn't a-bear to see made a fuss wi' like a Christian. An' the little ouzel must be washed, too, ivery Saturday, as if there wasn't children enoo to wash, wi'out washin' dogs.'

Now this particular morning it happened that Milly was quite too poorly to get up, and Mr Barton observed to Nanny, on going out, that he would call and tell Mr Brand to come. These circumstances were already enough to make Nanny anxious and susceptible. But the Countess, comfortably ignorant of them, came down as usual about eleven o'clock to her separate breakfast, which stood ready for her at that hour in the parlour; the kettle singing on the hob that she might make her own tea. There was a little jug of cream, taken according to custom from last night's milk, and specially saved for the Countess' breakfast. Jet always awaited his mistress at her bedroom door, and it was her habit to carry him downstairs.

'Now, my little Jet,' she said, putting him down gently on the hearthrug, 'you shall have a nice, nice breakfast.'

Jet indicated that he thought that observation extremely pertinent and well timed by immediately raising himself on his hind legs, and the Countess emptied the cream-jug into the saucer. Now there was usually a small jug of milk standing on the tray by the side of the cream, and destined for Jet's breakfast, but this morning Nanny, being 'moithered', had forgotten that part of the arrangements, so that when the Countess had made her tea, she perceived there was no second jug, and rang the bell. Nanny appeared, looking very red and heated – the fact was, she had been 'doing up' the kitchen fire, and that is a sort of work which by no means conduces to blandness of temper.

'Nanny, you have forgotten Jet's milk. Will you bring me some more cream, please?'

This was just a little too much for Nanny's forbearance.

'Yes, I dare say. Here am I wi' my hands full o' the children an' the dinner, and missis ill a-bed, and Mr Brand a-comin'; and I must run o'er the village to get more cream, 'cause you've give it to that nasty little blackamoor.'

'Is Mrs Barton ill?'

'Ill – yes – I should think she *is* ill, an' much you care. She's likely to be ill, moithered as *she* is from mornin' to night, wi' folks as had better be elsewhere.'

'What do you mean by behaving in this way?'

'Mean? Why I mean as the missis is a-slavin' her life out an' a-sittin' up o'nights, for folks as are better able to wait of *her*, i'stid o' lyin' a-bed an' doin' nothin' all the blessed day, but mek work.'

'Leave the room and don't be insolent.'

'Insolent! I'd better be insolent than like what some folks is, – a-livin' on other folks, an' bringin' a bad name on 'em into the bargain.'

Here Nanny flung out of the room, leaving the lady to digest this unexpected breakfast at her leisure.

The Countess was stunned for a few minutes, but when she began to recall Nanny's words, there was no possibility of avoiding very unpleasant conclusions from them, or of failing to see her position at the vicarage in an entirely new light. The interpretation, too, of Nanny's allusion to a 'bad name' did not lie out of the reach of the Countess' imagination, and she saw the necessity of quitting Shepperton without delay. Still, she would like to wait for her brother's letter – no – she would ask Milly to forward it to her – still better, she would go at once to London, enquire her brother's address at his banker's, and go to see him without preliminary.

She went up to Milly's room, and, after kisses and enquiries, said, 'I find, on consideration, dear Milly, from the letter I had yesterday, that I must bid you goodbye and go up to London at once. But you must not let me leave you ill, you naughty thing.'

'Oh no,' said Milly, who felt as if a load had been taken off her back, 'I shall be very well in an hour or two. Indeed, I'm much better now. You will want me to help you to pack. But you won't go for two or three days?'

'Yes, I must go tomorrow. But I shall not let you help me to pack, so don't entertain any unreasonable projects, but lie still. Mr Brand is coming, Nanny says.'

The news was not an unpleasant surprise to Mr Barton when he came home, though he was able to express more regret at the idea of parting than Milly could summon to her lips. He retained more of his original feeling for the Countess than Milly did, for women never betray themselves to men as they do to each other, and the Revd Amos had not a keen instinct for character. But he felt that he was being relieved from a difficulty, and in the way that was easiest for him. Neither he nor Milly suspected that it was Nanny who had cut the knot for them, for the Countess took care to give no sign on that subject. As for Nanny, she was perfectly aware of the relation between cause and effect in the affair, and secretly chuckled over her outburst of 'sauce' as the best morning's work she had ever done.

So, on Friday morning, a fly was seen standing at the vicarage gate with the Countess' boxes packed upon it, and presently that lady herself was seen getting into the vehicle. After a last shake of the hand to Mr Barton, and last kisses to Milly and the children, the door was closed; and as the fly rolled off, the little party at the vicarage gate caught a last glimpse of the handsome Countess leaning and waving kisses from the carriage window. Jet's little black phiz was also seen, and doubtless he had his thoughts and feelings on the occasion, but he kept them strictly within his own bosom.

The schoolmistress opposite witnessed this departure, and lost no time in telling it to the schoolmaster, who again communicated the news to the landlord of The Jolly Colliers at the close of the morning-school hours. Nanny poured the joyful tidings into the ear of Mr Farquhar's footman, who happened to call with a letter, and Mr Brand carried them to all the patients he visited that morning, after calling on Mrs Barton. So that, before Sunday, it was very generally known in Shepperton parish that the Countess Czerlaski had left the vicarage.

The Countess had left, but alas, the bills she had contributed to swell still remained; so did the exiguity of the children's clothing, which also was partly an indirect consequence of her presence; and so, too, did the coolness and alienation in the parishioners, which could not at once vanish before the fact of her departure. The Revd Amos was not exculpated – the past was not expunged. But what was worse than all, Milly's health gave frequent cause for alarm, and the prospect of baby's birth was overshadowed by more than the usual fears. The birth came prematurely, about six weeks after the Countess' departure, but Mr Brand gave favourable reports to all enquirers on the following day, which was Saturday. On Sunday, after morning service, Mrs Hackit called at the vicarage to enquire how Mrs Barton was, and was invited upstairs to see her. Milly lay placid and lovely in her feebleness, and held out her hand to Mrs Hackit with a beaming smile. It was very pleasant to her to see her old friend unreserved and cordial once more. The seven months' baby was very tiny and very red, but 'handsome is that handsome does' – he was pronounced to be 'doing well', and Mrs Hackit went home gladdened at heart to think that the perilous hour was over.

8

The following Wednesday, when Mr and Mrs Hackit were seated comfortably by their bright hearth, enjoying the long afternoon afforded by an early dinner, Rachel, the housemaid, came in and said, 'If you please 'm, the shepherd says, have you heard as Mrs Barton's wuss, and not expected to live?'

Mrs Hackit turned pale, and hurried out to question the shepherd, who, she found, had heard the sad news at an alehouse in the village. Mr Hackit followed her out and said, 'You'd better have the pony chaise, and go directly.'

'Yes,' said Mrs Hackit, too much overcome to utter any exclamations. 'Rachel, come an' help me on wi' my things.' When her husband was wrapping her cloak round her feet in the pony-chaise, she said, 'If I don't come home tonight, I shall send back the pony chaise, and you'll know I'm wanted there.'

'Yes, yes.'

It was a bright frosty day, and by the time Mrs Hackit arrived at the vicarage, the sun was near its setting. There was a carriage and pair standing at the gate, which she recognised as Dr Madeley's, the physician from Rotherby. She entered at the kitchen door that she might avoid knocking, and quietly question Nanny. No one was in the kitchen, but, passing on, she saw the sitting-room door open, and Nanny, with Walter in her arms, removing the knives and forks, which had been laid for dinner three hours ago.

'Master says he can't eat no dinner,' was Nanny's first word. 'He's never tasted nothin' sin' yesterday mornin', but a cup o' tea.'

'When was your missis took worse?'

'O' Monday night. They sent for Dr Madeley i' the middle o' the day yisterday, an' he's here again now.'

'Is the baby alive?'

'No, it died last night. The children's all at Mrs Bond's. She come and took 'em away last night, but the master says they must be fetched soon. He's upstairs now, wi' Dr Madeley and Mr Brand.'

At this moment Mrs Hackit heard the sound of a heavy, slow foot, in the passage, and presently Amos Barton entered, with dry, despairing eyes, haggard and unshaven. He expected to find the sitting-room as he left it, with nothing to meet his eyes but Milly's work-basket in the corner of the sofa, and the children's toys overturned in the bow-window. But when he saw Mrs Hackit come towards him with answering sorrow in her face, the pent-up fountain of tears was opened; he threw himself on the sofa, hid his face, and sobbed aloud.

'Bear up, Mr Barton,' Mrs Hackit ventured to say at last. 'Bear up, for the sake o' them dear children.'

'The children,' said Amos, starting up. 'They must be sent for. Someone must fetch them. Milly will want to…'

He couldn't finish the sentence, but Mrs Hackit understood him, and said, 'I'll send the man with the pony carriage for 'em.'

She went out to give the order, and encountered Dr Madeley and Mr Brand, who were just going.

Mr Brand said, 'I am very glad to see you are here, Mrs Hackit. No time must be lost in sending for the children. Mrs Barton wants to see them.'

'Do you quite give her up then?'

'She can hardly live through the night. She begged us to tell her how long she had to live; and then asked for the children.'

The pony carriage was sent, and Mrs Hackit, returning to Mr Barton, said she would like to go upstairs now. He went upstairs with her and opened the door. The chamber fronted the west; the sun was just setting, and the red light fell full upon the bed, where Milly lay with the hand of death visibly upon her. The feather bed had been removed, and she lay low on a mattress, with her head slightly raised by pillows. Her long fair neck seemed to be struggling with a painful effort; her features were pallid and pinched, and her eyes were closed. There was no one in the room but the nurse, and the mistress of the free school, who had come to give her help from the beginning of the change.

Amos and Mrs Hackit stood beside the bed, and Milly opened her eyes.

'My darling, Mrs Hackit is come to see you.'

Milly smiled and looked at her with that strange, far-off look which belongs to ebbing life.

'Are the children coming?' she said, painfully.

'Yes, they will be here directly.'

She closed her eyes again.

Presently the pony carriage was heard, and Amos, motioning to Mrs Hackit to follow him, left the room. On their way downstairs she suggested that the carriage should remain to take them away again afterwards, and Amos assented.

There they stood in the melancholy sitting-room – the five sweet children, from Patty to Chubby – all, with their mother's eyes – all, except Patty, looking up with a vague fear at their father as he entered. Patty understood the great sorrow that was come upon them, and tried to check her sobs as she heard her papa's footsteps.

'My children,' said Amos, taking Chubby in his arms, 'God is going to take away your dear mamma from us. She wants to see you to say goodbye. You must try to be very good and not cry.'

He could say no more, but turned round to see if Nanny was there with Walter, and then led the way upstairs, leading Dickey with the other hand. Mrs Hackit followed with Sophy and Patty, and then came Nanny with Walter and Fred.

It seemed as if Milly had heard the little footsteps on the stairs, for when Amos entered, her eyes were wide open, eagerly looking towards the door. They all stood by the bedside – Amos nearest to her, holding Chubby and Dickey. But she motioned for Patty to come first, and clasping the poor pale child by the hand, said, 'Patty, I'm going away from you. Love your papa. Comfort him, and take care of your little brothers and sisters. God will help you.'

Patty stood perfectly quiet, and said, 'Yes, Mamma.'

The mother motioned with her pallid lips for the dear child to lean towards her and kiss her; and then Patty's great anguish overcame her, and she burst into sobs. Amos drew her towards him and pressed her head gently to him, while Milly beckoned Fred and Sophy, and said to them more faintly, 'Patty will try to be your mamma when I am gone, my darlings. You will be good and not vex her.'

They leant towards her, and she stroked their fair heads, and kissed their tear-stained cheeks. They cried because Mamma was ill and Papa looked so unhappy; but they thought, perhaps next week things would be as they used to be again.

The little ones were lifted on the bed to kiss her. Little Walter said, 'Mamma, Mamma,' and stretched out his fat arms and smiled; and Chubby seemed gravely wondering, but Dickey, who had been looking fixedly at her, with lip hanging down, ever since he came into the room, now seemed suddenly pierced with the idea that Mamma was going away somewhere; his little heart swelled and he cried aloud.

Then Mrs Hackit and Nanny took them all away. Patty at first begged to stay at home and not go to Mrs Bond's again; but when Nanny reminded her that she had better go to take care of the younger ones, she submitted at once, and they were all packed in the pony carriage once more.

Milly kept her eyes shut for some time after the children were gone. Amos had sunk on his knees, and was holding her hand while he watched her face. By and by she opened her eyes, and, drawing him close to her, whispered slowly, 'My dear – dear – husband – you have been – very – good to me. You – have – made me – very – happy.'

She spoke no more for many hours. They watched her breathing becoming more and more difficult, until evening deepened into night, and until midnight was past. About half-past twelve she seemed to be trying to speak, and they leant to catch her words. 'Music – music – didn't you hear it?'

Amos knelt by the bed and held her hand in his. He did not

believe in his sorrow. It was a bad dream. He did not know when she was gone. But Mr Brand, whom Mrs Hackit had sent for before twelve o'clock, thinking that Mr Barton might probably need his help, now came up to him, and said, 'She feels no more pain now. Come, my dear sir, come with me.'

'She isn't *dead*?' shrieked the poor desolate man, struggling to shake off Mr Brand who had taken him by the arm. But his weary, weakened frame was not equal to resistance, and he was dragged out of the room.

9

They laid her in the grave – the sweet mother with her baby in her arms – while the Christmas snow lay thick upon the graves. It was Mr Cleves who buried her. On the first news of Mr Barton's calamity, he had ridden over from Tripplegate to beg that he might be made of some use, and his silent grasp of Amos' hand had penetrated like the painful thrill of life-recovering warmth to the poor benumbed heart of the stricken man.

The snow lay thick upon the graves, and the day was cold and dreary; but there was many a sad eye watching that black procession as it passed from the vicarage to the church, and from the church to the open grave. There were men and women standing in that churchyard who had bandied vulgar jests about their pastor, and who had lightly charged him with sin; but now, when they saw him following the coffin, pale and haggard, he was consecrated anew by his great sorrow, and they looked at him with respectful pity.

All the children were there, for Amos had willed it so, thinking that some dim memory of that sacred moment might remain even with little Walter, and link itself with what he would hear of his sweet mother in after-years. He himself led Patty and Dickey; then came Sophy and Fred; Mr Brand had begged to carry Chubby, and Nanny followed with Walter. They made a circle round the grave while the coffin was being lowered. Patty alone of all the children felt that Mamma was in that coffin, and that a new and sadder life had begun for Papa and herself. She was pale and trembling, but she clasped his hand more firmly as the coffin went down, and gave no sob. Fred and Sophy, though they were only two and three years younger, and though they had seen Mamma in her coffin, seemed to themselves to be looking at some strange show. They had not learnt to decipher that terrible handwriting of human destiny, illness and death. Dickey had rebelled against his black clothes, until he was told that it would be naughty to Mamma not to put them on, when he at once submitted; and now, though he had heard Nanny say that Mamma was in heaven, he had a vague notion that she would come home again tomorrow, and say he had been a good boy and let him empty her workbox. He stood close to his father, with great rosy cheeks, and wide-open blue eyes, looking first up at Mr Cleves and then down at the coffin, and thinking he and Chubby would play at that when they got home.

The burial was over, and Amos turned with his children to re-enter the house – the house where, an hour ago, Milly's dear body lay, where the windows were half darkened, and sorrow seemed to have a hallowed precinct for itself, shut out from the world. But now she was gone; the broad snow-reflected daylight was in all the rooms; the vicarage again seemed part of the common working-day world, and Amos, for the first time, felt that he was alone – that day after day, month after month, year after year, would have to be lived through without Milly's love. Spring would come, and she would not be there; summer, and she would not be there; and he would never have her again with him by the fireside in the long evenings. The seasons all seemed irksome to his thoughts; and how dreary the sunshiny days that would be sure to come! She was gone from him; and he could never show her his love any more, never make up for omissions in the past by filling future days with tenderness.

Oh the anguish of that thought that we can never atone to our dead for the stinted affection we gave them, for the light answers we returned to their plaints or their pleadings, for the little reverence we showed to that sacred human soul that lived so close to us, and was the divinest thing God had given us to know!

Amos Barton had been an affectionate husband, and while Milly was with him, he was never visited by the thought that perhaps his sympathy with her was not quick and watchful enough; but now he relived all their life together, with that terrible keenness of memory and imagination which bereavement gives, and he felt as if his very love needed a pardon for its poverty and selfishness.

No outward solace could counteract the bitterness of this inward woe. But outward solace came. Cold faces looked kind again, and parishioners turned over in their minds what they could best do to help their pastor. Mr Oldinport wrote to express his sympathy, and enclosed another twenty-pound note, begging that he might be permitted to contribute in this way to the relief of Mr Barton's mind from pecuniary anxieties, under the pressure of a grief which all his parishioners must share; and offering his interest towards placing the two eldest girls in a school expressly founded for clergymen's daughters. Mr Cleves succeeded in collecting thirty pounds among his richer clerical brethren, and, adding ten pounds himself, sent the sum to Amos, with the kindest and most delicate words of Christian fellowship and manly friendship. Miss Jackson forgot old grievances, and came to stay some months with Milly's children, bringing such material aid as she could spare from her small income. These were substantial helps which relieved Amos from the pressure of his money difficulties; and the friendly attentions, the kind pressure of the hand, the cordial looks he met with everywhere in his parish, made him feel that the fatal frost which had settled on his pastoral duties during the Countess' residence at the vicarage was completely thawed, and that the hearts of his parishioners were once more open to him.

No one breathed the Countess' name now, for Milly's memory hallowed her husband, as of old the place was hallowed on which an angel from God had alighted.

When the spring came, Mrs Hackit begged that she might have Dickey to stay with her, and great was the enlargement of Dickey's experience from that visit. Every morning he was allowed – being well wrapped up as to his chest by Mrs Hackit's own hands, but very bare and red as to his legs – to run loose in the cow and poultry yard, to persecute the turkeycock by satirical imitations of his gobble-gobble, and to put difficult questions to the groom as to the reasons why horses had four legs, and other transcendental matters. Then Mr Hackit would take Dickey up on horseback when he rode round his farm, and Mrs Hackit had a large plum cake in cut, ready to meet incidental attacks of hunger. So that Dickey had considerably modified his views as to the desirability of Mrs Hackit's kisses.

The Misses Farquhar made particular pets of Fred and Sophy, to whom they undertook to give lessons twice a week in writing and geography, and Mrs Farquhar devised many treats for the little ones. Patty's treat was to stay at home, or walk about with her papa, and when he sat by the fire in an evening, after the other children were gone to bed, she would bring a stool, and, placing it against his feet, would sit down upon it and lean her head against his knee. Then his hand would rest on that fair head, and he would feel that Milly's love was not quite gone out of his life.

So the time wore on till it was May again, and the church was quite finished and reopened in all its new splendour, and Mr Barton was devoting himself with more vigour than ever to his parochial duties. But one morning – it was a very bright morning, and evil tidings sometimes like to fly in the finest weather – there came a letter for Mr Barton, addressed in the vicar's handwriting. Amos opened it with some anxiety – somehow or other he had a presentiment of evil. The letter contained the announcement that Mr Carpe had resolved on coming to reside at Shepperton, and that, consequently, in six months from that time Mr Barton's duties as curate in that parish would be closed.

Oh, it was hard! Just when Shepperton had become the place where he most wished to stay – where he had friends who knew his sorrows – where he lived close to Milly's grave. To part from that grave seemed like parting with Milly a second time, for Amos was one who clung to all the material links between his mind and the past. His imagination was not vivid, and required the stimulus of actual perception.

It roused some bitter feeling, too, to think that Mr Carpe's wish to reside at Shepperton was merely a pretext for removing Mr Barton, in order that he might ultimately give the curacy of Shepperton to his own brother-in-law, who was known to be wanting a new position.

Still, it must be borne, and the painful business of seeking another curacy must be set about without loss of time. After the lapse of some months, Amos was obliged to renounce the hope of getting one at all near Shepperton, and he at length resigned himself to accepting one in a distant county. The parish was in a large manufacturing town where his walks would lie among noisy streets and dingy alleys, and where the children would have no garden to play in, no pleasant farmhouses to visit.

It was another blow inflicted on the bruised man.

10

At length the dreaded week was come when Amos and his children must leave Shepperton. There was general regret among the parishioners at his departure: not that any one of them thought his spiritual gifts pre-eminent, or was conscious of great edification from his ministry. But his recent troubles had called out their better sympathies, and that is always a source of love. Amos failed to touch the spring of goodness by his sermons, but he touched it effectually by his sorrows; and there was now a real bond between him and his flock.

'My heart aches for them poor motherless children,' said Mrs Hackit to her husband, 'a-going among strangers, and into a nasty town, where there's no good victuals to be had, and you must pay dear to get bad uns.'

Mrs Hackit had a vague notion of a town life as a combination of dirty backyards, measly pork, and dingy linen.

The same sort of sympathy was strong among the poorer class of parishioners. Old stiff-jointed Mr Tozer, who was still able to earn a little by gardening 'jobs', stopped Mrs Cramp, the charwoman, on her way home from the vicarage where she had been helping Nanny to pack up the day before the departure, and enquired very particularly into Mr Barton's prospects.

'Ah, poor mon,' he was heard to say, 'I'm sorry for un. He hedn't much here, but he'll be wuss off theer. Half a loaf's better nor ne'er un.'

The sad goodbyes had all been said before that last evening; and after all the packing was done and all the arrangements were made, Amos felt the oppression of that blank interval in which one has nothing left to think of but the dreary future – the separation from the loved and familiar, and the chilling entrance on the new and strange. In every parting there is an image of death.

Soon after ten o'clock, when he had sent Nanny to bed that she might have a good night's rest before the fatigues of the morrow, he stole softly out to pay a last visit to Milly's grave. It was a moonless night, but the sky was thick with stars, and their light was enough to show that the grass had grown long on the grave, and that there was a tombstone telling in bright letters, on a dark ground, that beneath were deposited the remains of Amelia, the beloved wife of Amos Barton, who died in the thirty-fifth year of her age, leaving a husband and six children to lament her loss. The final words of the inscription were, 'Thy will be done'.

The husband was now advancing towards the dear mound from which he was so soon to be parted, perhaps for ever. He stood a few minutes reading over and over again the words on the tombstone, as if to assure himself that all the happy and unhappy past was a reality. For love is frightened at the intervals of insensibility and callousness that encroach by little and little on the dominion of grief, and it makes efforts to recall the keenness of the first anguish.

Gradually, as his eye dwelt on the words, 'Amelia, the beloved wife,' the waves of feeling swelled within his soul, and he threw himself on the grave, clasping it with his arms, and kissing the cold turf.

'Milly, Milly, dost thou hear me? I didn't love thee enough – I wasn't tender enough to thee – but I think of it all now.' The sobs came and choked his utterance, and the warm tears fell.

CONCLUSION

Only once again in his life has Amos Barton visited Milly's grave. It was in the calm and softened light of an autumnal afternoon, and he was not alone. He held on his arm a young woman, with a sweet, grave face, which strongly recalled the expression of Mrs Barton's, but was less lovely in form and colour. She was about thirty, but there were some premature lines round her mouth and eyes, which told of early anxiety.

Amos himself was much changed. His thin circlet of hair was nearly white, and his walk was no longer firm and upright. But his glance was calm, and even cheerful, and his neat linen told of a woman's care. Milly did not take all her love from the earth when she died. She had left some of it in Patty's heart.

All the other children were now grown up, and had gone their several ways. Dickey, you will be glad to hear, had shown remarkable talents as an engineer. His cheeks are still ruddy, in spite of mixed mathematics, and his eyes are still large and blue; but in other respects his person would present no marks of identification for his friend Mrs Hackit, if she were to see him, especially now that her eyes must be grown very dim with the wear of more than twenty additional years. He is nearly six feet high, and has a proportionately broad chest; he wears spectacles, and rubs his large white hands through a mass of shaggy brown hair. But I am sure you have no doubt that Mr Richard Barton is a thoroughly good fellow, as well as a man of talent, and you will be glad any day to shake hands with him, for his own sake as well as his mother's.

Patty alone remains by her father's side, and makes the evening sunshine of his life.

NOTES

1. 'The New Police' refers to the London Police force established by Sir Robert Peel (1788–1850) in 1829 and other similar initiatives throughout the country in 1839; the Tithe Commutation Act was introduced in 1836 allowing people to convert a tenth of their produce into a fixed sum of money; the primitive postal service, the penny-post, was formed in 1840.

2. Thomas Sternhold (c.1500–1549) and John Hopkins (d.1570) composed the 1562 edition of metrical psalms, *The Whole Book of Psalms*, a new edition of which was introduced by Nicholas Brady (1659–1726) and Nahum Tate (1652–1715) in 1696. It was written as a result of the widely held belief that only words of Scripture should be sung in church, and was used well into the nineteenth century, the time when George Eliot was writing.

3. Various laws had been established during the Reformation preventing Catholics from holding public office, and the 'Catholic Question' was the on-going debate as to whether these should be repealed; the Catholic Emancipation Act was eventually introduced in 1829.

4. St Lawrence was martyred by being placed on an iron rack and slowly roasted over a fire.

5. A line from *The Task* (1784) by William Cowper (1731–1800).

6. Psalm 133.

7. Ranters were a fanatical sect of the seventeenth century; the name went on to become synonymous with any radical dissenters, especially the preachers of such sects.

8. The Religious Tract Society was established in 1799 to distribute pamphlets on a variety of spiritual and moral issues. It was closely associated with Evangelicals.

9. A type of silk, typically coarse-grained, originally from Naples.

10. Eleusis, near Athens, was typically the meeting-place for secret religious societies in ancient Greece; 'Eleusinian mysteries' refers to the rites celebrated there.

11. The free-thinker and radical Tom Paine (1737–1809) was the author of the controversial *The Rights of Man* (1791–2) and *The Age of Reason* (1793); his works proved an immense inspiration to nineteenth-century free-thinkers.

12. The 1834 New Poor Law addressed the problems surrounding the administration of relief to the poor; in particular, it called for chaplains to be appointed to workhouses.

13. The Revd Mr Johns perhaps refers to William Johns, a Unitarian minister; Mr Simeon to Charles Simeon (1759–1836), an admired Evangelical preacher and vicar of Trinity Church, Cambridge; John Newton (1725–1807) was a well-known Evangelical and hymn-writer; Thomas Scott (1747–1821) was an associate of John Newton and the author of a popular Bible commentary; the *Christian Observer*

was a moderate Church of England journal, with the *Record* being its Evangelical counterpart. This list of influences supports George Eliot's description of Barton as 'simply an evangelical clergyman'.

14. The 'Tractarian agitation' refers to the Oxford Movement (1833–45), led initially by John Henry Newman (1801–90), which resulted in the formation of a 'High-Church' movement in the Church of England. It was given the epithet 'Tractarian' due to its distribution of a series of tracts, many of which attacked 'Low-Church' beliefs.

15. The Socinians were an Anti-Trinitarian religious sect who followed the teachings of Lelio Sozzini (1525–62) and his nephew Fausto Sozzini (1539–1604) of Italy (Socinus is the Latinised form of their name); the Arimaspians were a mythical one-eyed people of Scythia who were constantly engaged in battle with the Gryphons, the guardians of gold.

16. John Jebb (1775–1833), Bishop of Limerick, produced a number of writings which anticipated many of the ideas of the Tractarians.

17. 'but, since it is sweet to gain a victory, / be bold! We shall be seen to be justified afterwards.' (Sophocles, *Philoctetes*, lines 81–2)

18. Eliot is referring to *Aeneid* IV.173–97 in which Virgil gives a description of Rumour.

19. A dialect word for 'skeleton'.

20. In Greek mythology, the husband of Alcmene and step-father of Heracles; Zeus took on his form to give a vast feast, giving rise to the proverbial use of the name Amphitryon to signify any rich and generous host.

21. A student who is 'plucked' is rejected for graduation on account of their poor examination results.

22. A glebe is land given to a clergyman as part of his living.

George Eliot was born Mary Ann Evans in Warwickshire in 1819. The youngest daughter of Robert Evans (a land agent) and Christina Pearson, she was a deeply religious child, and taught at Sunday school from the age of twelve. In 1828 she was sent to school in Nuneaton where she came under the influence of various Evangelicals, including the Revd John Edmund Jones, a preacher who would later appear in a number of her novels.

Following her mother's death in 1836, Mary Ann (now Marian) became her father's housekeeper and companion, but continued to educate herself in her spare time. In 1841 she moved to Coventry and became acquainted with the religious freethinkers Charles and Caroline Bray. Their influence on her caused her to question – and reject – much of her evangelical heritage, but the role of religion remained important to her and featured in many of her later works. Through the Brays, Marian was commissioned to translate Strauss's *Life of Jesus*, which appeared, anonymously, in 1846. As a result of this she met the publisher John Chapman who gave her a position on the *Westminster Review* in 1851. Around this time she moved to London and formed close friendships first with Herbert Spencer, who found her intimidating, and then with George Henry Lewes, with whom she lived until his death in 1878. The two never married as Lewes had previously married and had never divorced.

'The Sad Fortunes of the Reverend Amos Barton', the first of her *Scenes of Clerical Life*, appeared in *Blackwell's Magazine* in 1857 under the authorship of George Eliot; this was closely followed by 'Mr Gilfil's Love Story' and 'Janet's Repentance'. These were widely praised but speculation surrounded the identity of George Eliot, many supposing 'him' to be a clergyman. After much conjecture, she eventually stepped forward and revealed her identity.

Adam Bede appeared in 1859 and established her as a leading novelist of the day. This she followed up with *The Mill on the Floss* (1860) and *Silas Marner* (1861). *Middlemarch*, considered by many to be her masterpiece, was published in instalments in 1871–2, and *Daniel Deronda* in 1874–6. With these behind her, she was hailed as the greatest living novelist, and counted Henry James, Ralph Waldo Emerson, Ivan Turgenev, and Queen Victoria among her admirers.

In 1878 Lewes died and Eliot formed a new attachment, marrying the forty-year-old John Walter Cross in 1880. This relationship distressed many of her friends, but brought about reconciliation with her brother Isaac with whom she had been estranged since 1857. Not long after her marriage, however, she died and, in 1882, was buried alongside Lewes.

HESPERUS PRESS – 100 PAGES

Hesperus Press, as suggested by the Latin motto, is committed to bringing near what is far – far both in space and time. Works written by the greatest authors, and unjustly neglected or simply little known in the English-speaking world, are made accessible through new translations and a completely fresh editorial approach. Through these short classic works, each around 100 pages in length, the reader will be introduced to the greatest writers from all times and all cultures.

For more information on Hesperus Press, please visit our website: **www.hesperuspress.com**

ET REMOTISSIMA PROPE

SELECTED TITLES FROM HESPERUS PRESS

Gustave Flaubert *Memoirs of a Madman*

Alexander Pope *Scriblerus*

Ugo Foscolo *Last Letters of Jacopo Ortis*

Anton Chekhov *The Story of a Nobody*

Joseph von Eichendorff *Life of a Good-for-nothing*

Mark Twain *The Diary of Adam and Eve*

Giovanni Boccaccio *Life of Dante*

Victor Hugo *The Last Day of a Condemned Man*

Joseph Conrad *Heart of Darkness*

Edgar Allan Poe *Eureka*

Emile Zola *For a Night of Love*

Daniel Defoe *The King of Pirates*

Giacomo Leopardi *Thoughts*

Nikolai Gogol *The Squabble*

Franz Kafka *Metamorphosis*

Herman Melville *The Enchanted Isles*

Leonardo da Vinci *Prophecies*

Charles Baudelaire *On Wine and Hashish*

William Makepeace Thackeray *Rebecca and Rowena*

Wilkie Collins *Who Killed Zebedee?*

Théophile Gautier *The Jinx*

Charles Dickens *The Haunted House*

Luigi Pirandello *Loveless Love*

Fyodor Dostoevsky *Poor People*

E.T.A. Hoffmann *Mademoiselle de Scudéri*

Henry James *In the Cage*

Francis Petrarch *My Secret Book*

André Gide *Theseus*

D.H. Lawrence *The Fox*

Percy Bysshe Shelley *Zastrozzi*

Marquis de Sade *Incest*

Oscar Wilde *The Portrait of Mr W.H.*

Giacomo Casanova *The Duel*

Leo Tolstoy *Hadji Murat*

Friedrich von Schiller *The Ghost-seer*

Nathaniel Hawthorne *Rappaccini's Daughter*

Pietro Aretino *The School of Whoredom*

Honoré de Balzac *Colonel Chabert*

Thomas Hardy *Fellow-Townsmen*

Arthur Conan Doyle *The Tragedy of the Korosko*

Stendhal *Memoirs of an Egotist*

Katherine Mansfield *In a German Pension*

Giovanni Verga *Life in the Country*

Ivan Turgenev *Faust*

Theodor Storm *The Lake of the Bees*

F. Scott Fitzgerald *The Rich Boy*

Dante Alighieri *New Life*

Guy de Maupassant *Butterball*

Charlotte Brontë *The Green Dwarf*

Elizabeth Gaskell *Lois the Witch*

Joris-Karl Huysmans *With the Flow*

Gabriele D'Annunzio *The Book of the Virgins*

Alexander Pushkin *Dubrovsky*

Heinrich von Kleist *The Marquise of O–*